THE SERPENT

SERPENT

THE SERPENT

DAVID DRAKE

THE SERPENT

This is a work of fiction. All the characters and events portr
fictional, and any resemblance to real people or incidents i

ayed in this book are
s purely coincidental.

rtions thereof

Copyright © 2021 by David Drake

All rights reserved, including the right to reproduce this book or po
in any form.

A Baen Books Original

Baen Publishing Enterprises
P.O. Box 1403
Riverdale, NY 10471
www.baen.com

ISBN: 978-1-9821-2557-8

Art by Todd Lockwood

First printing, July 2021

Distributed by Simon & Schuster
1230 Avenue of the Americas
New York, NY 10020

Library of Congress Cataloging-in-Publication Data

Names: Drake, David, 1945– author.
Title: The serpent / David Drake.
Description: Riverdale, NY : Baen, [2021] | Series: Time of heroes ; volume
   3
Identifiers: LCCN 2021018949 | ISBN 9781982125578 (hardcover)
Subjects: GSAFD: Fantasy fiction. | Science fiction.
Classification: LCC PS3554.R196 S46 2021 | DDC 813/.54—dc23
LC record available at https://lccn.loc.gov/2021018949

Pages by Joy Freeman (www.pagesbyjoy.com)
Printed in the United States of America
10 9 8 7 6 5 4 3 2 1

To Marcia Decker

Proof that a feminist isn't required to respond with screaming rage when faced with a differing viewpoint

AUTHOR'S NOTE

The Serpent is based on the legendry of King Arthur as were *The Spark* and *The Storm*. Much of the action is adapted from the romances of Chretien de Troyes and the Prose Lancelot. These provided plot points, but more important was the *feel* of what went into a medieval romance.

Besides those sources directly in the Matter of Britain (to use the term of Jean Bodin) I also used *The Knight in Pantherskin*, an Armenian epic of the twelfth century. There are Armenian castles in the neighborhood of Adana, Turkey, and I was privileged to visit one when we were visiting friends there. The world is full of wonderful things, especially if you're willing to broaden your horizon to regions and subjects which are off the beaten track. When you visit a castle you get a feeling for why it was built there which a map only suggests.

I suppose what I'm saying is that fiction isn't divorced from reality, but that it should emphasize an emotional response over facts and logic.

For the first time in this series I incorporated scenes from Ariosto's *Orlando Furioso*. There are wonderful vivid scenes in the work, but to my surprise there is very little plot and I was reading it for connected plot. This is a useful reminder for any writer: action is not story.

Some while ago I titled an RCN novel: *In the Stormy Red S' y*. The title was from "The Voyage of Maeldune," a poem of Alf ed, Lord Tennyson. Tennyson had read an Irish epic which sur ives in a twelfth-century form but probably goes back to the eighth

vii

century. I went back to the Irish work, *The Voyage of Mael Duin*, for inspiration. It wasn't as complete a model as I'd have liked because it involved a boatload of adventurers, rather than one or two, but it did provide vivid scenes.

I incorporated elements from *Flemish Legends*, compiled by Charles de Coster and *A Book of Danish Ballads* by Axel Olrik, to get a pre-literary feel to my work.

Dave Drake
david-drake.com

THE SERPENT

In our great hall there stood a vacant chair,
Fashioned by Merlin ere he past away,
And carven with strange figures; and in and out
The figures, like a serpent, ran a scroll
Of letters in a tongue no man could read.
And Merlin called it "The Siege Perilous,"
Perilous for good and ill...

—*The Holy Grail*
Alfred, Lord Tennyson

CHAPTER 1

Two Weeks Out of Dun Add

The color of the Waste to either side of the Road had changed from muddy brown to something closer to gray/blue. Apparent color, of course, and even that had been translated through the eyes of my dog Sam.

From the corners of my eyes the Waste looked like the reeds glimpsed from a causeway through a marsh. If I tried to look squarely at it, there was nothing really to see—which was the true state of affairs. Still the change in what my brain thought it was seeing meant something. I turned and called to my servant following a pace behind me, "Baga, is it Boyd's Node we're coming to?"

"No, boss, that's the second node on in this reach," Baga said. "Then a couple uninhabited ones."

Mistress Toledana, the Clerk of Here, had provided us with a full itinerary before we left Dun Add fourteen days ago. I'd made a serious attempt to memorize it. I didn't doubt that Baga was correct, though. He was a boatman, which is a different kind of mind from mine and maybe it was better tuned to distances and directions than mine was.

On the other hand, I was a warrior who could operate the weapons of the Ancients. Also I was a Maker and could in a trance repair the tools the Ancients had left in this shattered Cosmos. I didn't have the natural skill for weapons which the greatest warriors like Lord Clain did, but because I understood

1

weapons better than most warriors, I could use them to the limits of their power without exceeding it. I had also learned to use Sam's ability to predict motion better than any human could, which was a trick that I thought any warrior should be able to learn.

Very few had, however. As a result I was one of the most respected members of Lord Jon's Hall of Champions. A status which my size and strength would not have earned me.

The entrance to the node looked like a black stripe in the Waste from the Road, which meant that it got a fair amount of traffic. Contact points between the Road and nodes of Here grew closed slowly if they were not used. Even stretches of the Road squeezed shut.

I guided Sam toward the line which became a gauze curtain for an instant as my feet stepped once more on firm ground. I had returned to Here. Landingplace in this node didn't rise to formalities like the clerk or steward of the most populous places, but at the edge of the grassed clearing was a canvas tilt covering a rough table on which sat half a dozen jacks of tarred leather. A cask sat on trestles at the back and a boy hopped to his feet beside it when Sam and I appeared.

"Ale, sirs?" the boy asked. "Or if you want a dram, Oscar right in town has some righteous gin! A lot better than what you'll find at the Cowbell and that's the other end of town besides."

I was going to pass on, but Baga said, "I'm pretty dry, Master?"

"What do you charge for a stoup?" I asked the boy. "And what's this place called anyway? Not Boyd, is it?"

"Boyd's is the next one left up the Road," the boy said. "This is Winslow. It's three coppers for the pair of you. And I can pour a pan of water free for your dog."

"We'll do that," I said, though it wasn't cheap. The bronze points I counted out ran twelve to the silver Rider in Dun Add—but I wasn't in Dun Add. The price wouldn't have been robbery back home in Beune, though we mainly got along by barter because Beune gets bloody few strangers passing through.

"I suppose you're here for the mummy?" the boy said after filling the jacks.

"What mummy?" I said. The ale was good but nothing I'd have hiked to the next node for, let alone come fourteen days out. The thought reminded me and I took out the little tablet in which I was jotting notes to give the Clerk of Here when I got back to Dun Add. Jon was determined to bring all Mankind into the Commonwealth, but that meant mapping it for administrative purposes.

Administration didn't mean only taxes, but it certainly meant taxes. The apparatus of law and order are expensive to create and maintain. Not everybody is going to agree with Jon's priorities. I knew him well enough to be sure that Jon really meant the best for everybody, but some folks would certainly disagree, some of them violently. The violent ones ran into Champions of Mankind like me. The Champions' job was to bring disagreements to Dun Add where they could be settled by a court.

We were chosen from folk who could settle fights ourselves if a party insisted on pushing the matter, however.

"A peddler came by last week," the boy said. "He'd been prospecting in the Waste for Ancient artifacts to sell to Makers, there's people who do that, you know?"

"I know," I said. I'd done it myself when I was a kid on Beune; mostly for my own use, though, rather than for sale.

"Well, right up the Road from here he found a whole body of some guy who'd got lost in the Waste and died there. He borrowed a hand cart from Nonce who owns the Cowbell and brought it in. It was dry like a dead bird that's been lying on a roof all year. Nonce bought it from him for silver and he has it on display in the common room in a glass case that he charges two coppers to take the curtains off."

"What!" I said. "Did the prospector who found the mummy know what Nonce planned?"

"Hell if I know!" the kid said. "Guess he did, though. What else could Nonce have planned after paying money for the thing? And it was dead anyhow."

"*It,* as you call him, was a human being, a prospector a lot like the fellow who found him!" I said. A lot like *me,* was what I was really thinking. I strode up the path through a screen of spiky brush. I left my weapon and shield in my pockets, though I could have them out in a heartbeat if I needed them.

Jon's Champions all had top-quality hardware, some of it better than mine. Mine, however, were uniquely compact. Most warriors wore harnesses to support their hardware. My shield and weapon fit comfortably in the pockets of a normal, loose-fitting tunic. The disadvantage was that taking them out was immediately threatening in a fashion that an armed warrior was not.

The houses of Winslow had heavily stuccoed walls and thatched roofs. A couple of dogs barked as I strode up the street but nobody came over to try conclusions with Sam. He didn't bark back. He could sense my mood and knew that we were at work though my shield and weapon weren't live yet.

The tavern at the end of the street had a large wooden silhouette of a cowbell rather than simply a real bell. There were three loungers on the bench outside. "Where's Nonce?" I said when one of them looked up as I approached.

"Who wants to know?" a different lounger responded.

"The Commonwealth of Mankind!" I said. I brought out my gear though I didn't switch it on yet. The loungers leaped up as though the bench had become a grill on a hot fire. Baga pulled the door open for me so that I didn't have to pocket the shield or weapon to free a hand.

The interior was lighted by an eight-paned window in the end wall to the left. The fireplace was to the right, and the bar faced me. Under the window was a box resting on two sawbucks and covered by what seemed to be a dark towel.

"You've come to see the mummy, sirs?" asked the bald man behind the bar. There were half a dozen in the common room all told. The pair standing in the fireplace nook seemed to be travellers; the rest were local.

I nodded to Baga, who whisked the towel away. The man behind the bar said, "That'll be five coppers, sirs. Since you're a gentleman, that's five for you and your servant both."

I looked into the box. I'd seen mummies from the Waste. The skin blackens and all the moisture is drawn out of the flesh so that it wraps the bones in a thin coating that could almost be paint.

The tendons shrink also, so the corpse was in a fetal position with his knees and arms tight against his chest. I say "his" because I've never met a woman who prospected in the Waste. The facial features were no more evident than those of a skull.

"This was a human being!" I said to Nonce. "He was working at one of the most unpleasant and dangerous jobs a man can do, probably scraping a bare living for himself and his family. You do not make him a spectacle because his luck ran out!"

"And who are you to say that?" Nonce demanded. His hand found the mallet he used to set bungs in fresh casks, but he wasn't fool enough to openly threaten an armed man.

"I'm Pal of Beune, a member of the Leader's Hall of Champions," I said. "I order you in the name of the Commonwealth to give this poor devil a proper burial!"

"Well, what about the money I paid for it?" Nonce said, now plaintively rather than threatening.

"Baga," I said. "Toss him a silver piece. And out of that," I added, gesturing toward Nonce with my weapon, "you'll pay for the burial. He was a man, like you and me, Nonce. Remember that."

Every time I went into the Waste I thought of what would happen if I got lost and couldn't find my way back to Here. There are no wayposts in the Waste and you could wander forever in it if you missed your direction even slightly as you tried to return. Unless you found a node or a stretch of the Road, you would wander until you overheated and died.

As this unknown prospector had done an unknown number of years ago.

"I didn't know there was some law about bodies you find in the Waste," Nonce said. "I guess you folk in Dun Add are just too highfalutin for us common folks out in the sticks."

"I think common decency is pretty much the same everywhere," I said, "and you're the first person I've met who thinks Beune is highfalutin. Anyway you'd better get moving on burying the fellow. Do you have a priest here on Winslow?"

"We bloody well do not!" Nonce said.

Another of the local men said, "Oscar at the Flower is a lay preacher. He could say a few words—if you want that, milord?"

"I do want that," I said. "That's the other tavern we came past? Baga, go fetch Oscar up to do the honors if he would." I looked at Nonce and added, "I'll pay him if he charges for this kind of thing."

"Look, it's a dead body and no kin to any of us," Nonce said. "Or to you either so far as I can see."

Baga had gone off at a trot. I took a closer look at the corpse, wondering what he'd been thinking in his last minutes.

All his clothing had crumbled away. If he'd had a collecting bag, it was dust in the Waste now. The man who'd found him and brought him in had been a prospector himself, so he'd probably done what I would have if I'd found the corpse: searched the surface around the body for artifacts the dead man might have been carrying when he died.

I looked at the mummy's clenched fists. The right hand was a noticeably larger ball than the left; though that might have been a whim of the way the body had dried out. Still...

I began to unroll the mummy's fingers. I thought they might break but they instead opened like leather straps which had not dried hard.

They were gripping something as I'd guessed. It was a short rod with bristles of another metal set at right angles near one end in the fashion of a toothbrush. The barrel was carved with a snake and the design filled with silver wire. I'd have to go into a Maker's trance to be sure of what the precise composition was but the rod appeared to be iron, and the bristles a mix of noble metals.

"What's that?" Nonce demanded.

A strictly honest answer would have been "Damned if I know," but that wouldn't have shut the innkeeper up. I said, "Business for Master Louis, the great Maker who builds weapons for the Leader, Jon."

"It's a *weapon*?" said Nonce, jerking back the hand that had started to reach for the object.

I dropped it into my belt purse. "That'll be for Louis to decide," I said. "Or maybe Jon himself."

I would certainly give it a thorough trance examination when I had leisure. At the moment I wasn't even sure it was an Ancient artifact, though I thought it was.

"Say," called older of the travellers in the fireplace nook; the fire wasn't lighted at this time of year, of course. "If you're one of Jon's Champions, I guess you'd know Lord Frobier, wouldn't you?"

"I do," I said. "We're not close."

Frobier was stuck up beyond the norm of Champions of Mankind—and as a group we tend to think pretty well of ourselves. Some of the better-off farmers on Beune weren't a lot better. It's just the way some people are.

"I figured you must 'cause there's not so many of you, is there?" the old man said. His younger companion was obviously trying to shush him, probably because he didn't like the idea of calling the attention of an armed stranger to themselves. "Anyway, Frobier's up on Boyd's Node right now."

"What in the name of goodness is he doing out here?" I said. What with retirements and deaths on the one hand and successful Aspirants on the other, you could never be sure how many Champions there were in the Hall at any one time, but it wasn't going more than a hundred for sure. Finding two of us this close together was a greater surprise to me than it obviously was to the old man.

"He's not doing much at all," the old man said. "He got sick like to die. His cook told me he was on the mend now, but last week when they arrived on Boyd they didn't figure he'd make it."

"What happened to him?" I asked, but the traveller just shrugged.

Baga came in just then with a paunchy middle-aged man in tow. "This is Master Oscar," he said to me.

"Baga," I said. "I need to get to Boyd's Node in a hurry. Do you need to catch a meal first?"

He shrugged. "I guess I can wait a couple hours if you're in a hurry," he said. "You want to head right on out?"

"If you're okay with that," I said, stepping past him to the door. Sam was out as soon as I had the panel open a crack.

Over my shoulder I called, "Nonce! When I come back through, you'd best have that poor prospector buried. You hear me?"

I don't know for sure that he answered. I didn't even know for sure that I'd survive to come back.

CHAPTER 2

Champion of Mankind

We reached Boyd's Node quickly but to my surprise we had to hike over a mile to reach the inn where Lord Frobier was staying. Three separate branches of the Road met at Boyd's Node, as they did at Dun Add, but at Dun Add the branches connected just outside the node itself with only a short stub into the node. At Boyd's the three branches entered Here separately, and Lord Frobier had entered at the community called Eastown.

The track between it and South, where we'd come in, was decent for Here and it hadn't rained recently, though it was nowhere near as good a surface as that of the Road (whatever that was). The innkeeper at South was resentfully aware of Frobier, who'd arrived with a party of almost twenty. "I *never* have luck like that!"

That seemed like a large group to me also, though I knew Frobier travelled with an entourage of servants befitting his stature as a Champion.

Baga could cook and carry the slight paraphernalia I needed on the Road—dried food and a tilt or ground sheet in case we had to camp on a completely uninhabited node. I was from Beune, which gave me nothing to brag about. Anybody who questioned my status as a Champion could meet me on the field and I would prove it on his body. There were better warriors than I but bloody few of them. And Lord Frobier wasn't one of the exceptions.

The inn at Eastown was a big stone-built structure with a loft which was probably high enough in the front for men to walk upright. I thought the common room in the front of the ground floor would be crowded with a party of twenty staying there as I'd heard, but in fact the tapster was alone with two servants in violet tunics who must be Frobier's men.

I walked in ahead of Sam and Baga. "I came to see Lord Frobier," I said, addressing the room.

"Lord Pal?" said the short, foxy servant whom I vaguely recalled from Dun Add. "His Lordship is upstairs and your visit will be very welcome, I'm sure. Let me go up and tell his lordship you're here."

The inn had a proper staircase instead of just a ladder to the loft. The servant skipped up it while the tapster looked at me. "Will you be needing lodging for yourself and your man, milord?" he asked.

"Probably," I said. "We'll want a meal regardless. Baga, stable Sam and I'll be back as soon as I've talked to Frobier."

I went up the stairs with less enthusiasm than the servant had; it was going for a long day. At the head of the stairs was a hallway which four doors opened off. The servant stood in the doorway of one of those serving the front half of the loft. I joined him and saw Frobier stretched out on a low bed woven of rye straw.

The windows on this side were low and Frobier's complexion may not have really been as yellow as I thought at first glance, but his cheeks were certainly sunken and though the basin beside the head of the bed had been emptied, the stench of vomit clung to it.

"Did Jon send you to replace me?" Frobier said. If his voice had been stronger, I think he'd have shouted.

"I was patrolling in this region and heard you were laid up," I said. "Were you on routine patrol also, Frobier?"

That surprised me, because I'd asked Mistress Toledana to plot me a route which hadn't been covered recently. I'm a strong believer in Champions making routine patrols. The courts at Dun Add provided justice for citizens who came to the capital to judge between them and a neighbor. That was better for the Commonwealth and generally for the parties themselves than letting them decide the rights of the matter by force.

A Champion passing through a region could often save the parties a long and expensive journey while still arriving at a neutral assessment. Apart from solving conflicts, though, the Commonwealth was aided just by Champions passing through nodes and reminding citizens that the Commonwealth existed as more than a taxing authority.

"I've got better things to do than wander through the boondocks!" Frobier said with a snort. That had been too enthusiastic and he lurched up in a coughing fit. After he wiped his mouth with a rag he said, "Lord Ercole of Banft is marrying his daughter, Lady Irene, to Lord Diederich of Hume. Ercole hired guards to protect Irene on the journey, but Ercole wanted a Champion to go with her as befit her rank. Jon tapped me for the assignment, but here on Boyd I was taken suddenly ill."

I glanced over my shoulder to make sure what the movement I heard was; Frobier's chubby servant was coming up the stairs to join us. "Where's Lady Irene, then?" I asked.

"How in blazes would I know?" Frobier demanded. "I told you I was sick!"

The servant who'd just come up said, "The lady went off with her guards after the master took sick. She said she didn't need to wait. That was two days ago, milord!"

"The Lady Irene is a self-willed bitch so that doesn't surprise me at all," Frobier said. "And she didn't like men! I don't envy Lord Diederich—if she even gets there."

"What do you mean 'If she gets there'?" I said. "What's going to prevent her?"

"Hell if I know," Frobier said. "She went off on her own without bothering even to tell me on my bed. I sure wouldn't trust my daughter with that rascal Errol."

"He was captain of the guards," the foxy servant said to me. "The master's surely right on that."

"Look," I said to Frobier. "It looks to me like Errol or another guard poisoned you to get Lady Irene away. I'll help you get her back but I think we've got to move fast."

"That can't be," Frobier said. "I've heard you're a wise-ass, Pal, but you better butt out of this one until you at least learn something about it. Jorome here—" he gestured to the plumper servant "—cooked all my meals."

"And before you get a silly notion about me, your lordship," the cook said, "Lord Frobier ate all his meals with Lady Irene and she was right as rain the morning she left."

"That's right," Frobier said. "And if she was in such a hurry to get away, then she earned whatever she gets, *I* think."

Lord Jon wouldn't think that, I was sure; but Jon wasn't here and it wouldn't make the current situation any better if I said that. Baga came up the stairs and the tapster called past him to say, "Tell your master I've got a cold joint for your supper."

"Is there anything you need from me, Frobier?" I said.

"I didn't need you to be here," he said. "I don't know now why you've come."

"I'll stop troubling you and have my dinner," I said and left the room, taking Baga back down the steps with me. "I'll take a room after all," I said to the tapster. "Don't guess we'll be going out till the morning."

We were eating mutton and kale and the tapster—the host—Grigor even had provided a mustard pot. I was just about to praise Grigor for the quality of the food when the front door opened and a fellow not much older than I am came in. "Good day, sir," Grigor said. "You'll want a room?"

"I'm Master Timmons," the fellow said. "I'm a clerk on my way to Dun Add to join the Leader's government."

He wore a weapon and shield. At a glance at them in fabric holsters, I couldn't give a detailed analysis of their quality but the weapon struck me as pretty low-end and the shield no better than the one I'd made for myself in Beune using an Ancient umbrella as my starting point.

That shield was crap and I got the tar whaled out of me the first time I jousted with it. On the other hand the fact that I was armed had kept me safe along the Road to Dun Add, and I supposed that was all that Timmons required. I'd hoped to become a Champion of Mankind; Timmons only wanted to push paper in Jon's growing bureaucracy, which he might be well suited for.

"Yes, I'd like lodging and a meal for my companion and myself," Timmons said. He moved slightly and I saw for the first time the woman behind him in the doorway.

She was brown-haired and ordinary; not bad looking, but I've been living in Dun Add where women strive to be glamorous. This woman would have stood out in Beune but she would have to change a good deal to be comfortable in the capital. The women there would tear her to shreds. She would get as little sympathy as a hick like me had received from the men when I hiked to Dun Add to become a Champion.

Grigor brightened when he saw her, however. "Ah! Mistress Clara," he said. "Will her ladyship be joining us shortly?"

"I've left Lady Irene," the maid said.

"Really," said Timmons, looking at Clara, "she left you."

To the rest of us he explained, "I'm on my way from Messageries to Dun Add and I stopped at the node just up from here and met the party. There's nothing there but ruins and desert but Lady Irene had stopped with Mistress Clara and her guards."

"That's not on the route to Banft," I said "They'd have had to go out the way we came in, at South to get the Road for Banft."

"Madame didn't want to go to Banft," Clara said. "She'd bribed Errol to take her to her cousin in Westbriggan but I heard the guards talking. They were going to sell her a long way from here, a node that isn't in the Commonwealth. Only instead she just disappeared, the way she used to do back home on Banft when she was helping Master Sans for her father."

"Mistress Clara was left on her own," Timmons said. "I was glad to offer my protection to get her to Dun Add."

"But what about Lady Irene?" I asked.

"I scarcely think she is any of my business," Timmons said stiffly.

"A women left in the middle of a pack of wolves is any man's business!" I said, then regretted I'd been so hot.

In all truth, Timmons wasn't a man in the fashion I meant the word. I'd been in the Hall of Champions, but it was more than that. When I was a kid I'd wallowed in heroic romances. I'd formed myself on those models.

When I reached Dun Add I realized that the reality behind those romances was a harsh one. That hadn't really changed me, though: the truth of what men and heroes did was much less inspiring than the romances, but I still preferred the romance and guided my choices by it.

Most men made much more practical choices, as they certainly ought to do. I basically tried to do as a romantic hero would whenever I was faced with a choice. It's what worked for me.

"Well, I'm not standing in your way," the clerk said haughtily.

"He's right, Baga," I said. "You and I are back on the Road

as soon as we have Sam out of the stables. Can somebody here point me in the right direction, Grigor?"

"I'll take you back," said Clara, "if Master Timmons will come along with the dog so I can get back?"

Timmons nodded. "All right," he said. "Errol and his thugs are a bad lot, no mistake." He looked at me and added, "I think you're a fool, sir, and I will not throw my life away with you. But I'll see you're on the right path if that's really what you want to do."

Timmons's dog was more terrier than not. I took a glance through her eyes and found her view of the Road adequate, though I didn't have the rapport with her that I did with Sam. Human eyes unaided don't see the Road, though mica lenses can provide a workable crutch for folks who need to leave Here and don't have a trained animal to link with.

Timmons and Clara had found their way to Boyd once, so there was really no reason for me to be concerned about them finding their way back after pointing me in the right direction. I did anyway, maybe to keep myself from worrying about what was going to happen after I found Errol and his gang.

"I been with Lady Irene ten years," Clara said to me. "She was always an odd one, but it wasn't a problem being her maid. It was just the way she was raised by Master Sans. He's a Maker and he's real close with Lord Ercole, her father."

"What about her mother?" I asked. Clara was walking with me instead of with Timmons, who was leading. I don't know what he thought about the business, but I suspected Clara was only a convenience for a few nights so far as he was concerned. She'd already forced him to get more involved in the business than he'd intended to be.

"She died when Irene was born," Clara said. "That's what they told me, anyway. Master Sans took her off and raised her until she was about eight and Sans brought her back to Banft and Ercole hired me."

"That's crazy!" I said. "I've never heard of a parent behaving that way!"

Clara shrugged. "You can't blame her for being a bit strange, you see."

Ercole had to be a powerful noble to have gotten a Champion

to escort his daughter, and men like that—especially those living at a considerable distance from Dun Add—were apt to be self-willed. What Clara had described was pretty extreme, though.

"I said Sans was close to Ercole," Clara went on. "His lordship didn't take another woman after his wife died, but Irene brought back dolls for Ercole from wherever Sans was. He'd gone somewhere, but he sent Irene back with the dolls. They only lived a couple months but Irene always went and brought back another."

"Were the dolls machines that Master Sans was making?" I said. Since I'd been living at Dun Add I'd seen plenty of men who were likely to be with a different woman every few weeks. My friend Morseth was a lot that way himself to tell the truth. It wasn't the way I'd been raised to think was right, but he was my friend regardless. He didn't knock the women around—I wouldn't hang around with him if he had—but he went off them pretty quick.

"They were alive," Clara said flatly. "They didn't live long but they were alive.

"The last one died six months ago," she said. "Lady Irene went away like usual, but when she came back she didn't bring a doll. That was when Lord Ercole decided to marry her off."

"Did she want to be married?" I asked.

"No," Clara said, "but her father didn't pay any attention to her before, and he didn't now either. He got a good settlement from Lord Diederich and he packed her off to Hume. And me too, of course."

She looked sideways at me and said, "I wonder what it's going to be like living in Dun Add?"

"I don't know," I said. "I come from a place called Beune, too small for you to ever hear of. And I guess it'll be different for a girl anyhow."

That was true even if Timmons supported her for at least a little while after they arrived. There were a lot of things in this world that I didn't think were right, but I couldn't change most of them. And not everybody shared my opinions, anyway.

Timmons stopped and turned to face us at a fork in the Road. "You'll take the left way, then," he said. "It's not as far to where Errol was as it'll take us to go back to Boyd and finally get a meal.

"Clara," he said in a harsher voice. "Come along right now unless you want to stay here."

The maid looked at me; hopefully, I thought. "She's going back with you," I said. "I don't know how this is going to go, but it's no place for her. Come along, Baga. We're going to meet some people."

Sam started up the branch without me even touching him. You and your dog get that way pretty quick, especially if you've fought together. Which we were likely to be doing again shortly. The hairs on the back of Sam's neck were starting to bristle so he was smelling my expectations in my sweat.

"Going to get your hardware out, sir?" Baga asked as we strode along.

"Not until we've met these other folks," I said. "If I walk in on them tooled up, they've got to fight. And I'd rather not if I don't have to."

"You're going to have to, boss," Baga said. I was pretty sure he was right.

We reached a blotch in the Waste which marked the Road's conjunction with a node. I said to Baga, "You can wait on the Road if you like."

"And if they scrag you, do what?" he said. "Or did you figure to leave Sam out here too? Go on, boss. I said I was with you, didn't I?"

We walked through the hazy barrier into a node which must once have been a city but which had been overtaken by waves of reddish sand. Walls and columns were visible for as far as I could see, except where the dunes were at their highest.

A group of men clustered near a campfire. They'd either have packed in the wood or found the corpse of a desiccated tree overwhelmed by the sand. There were at least a dozen of them and a group of dogs interspersed among them.

"Good day, masters," I called as I walked toward the group. The nearest of the men was ten feet away. The dogs had started up and several began yapping; Sam ignored them like the trained professional he was.

"I'm looking for a missing woman," I said. My arms were loose by my sides. "Lady Irene of Banft. Have any of you seen her?"

Along with the dogs, several men had jumped to their feet also. One of them was a fellow well over six feet tall with red hair. "Diccon," he ordered. "See him off!"

The man closest to me was a teenager with wispy hair. He drew his weapon and shield and stepped toward me. The hardware was no great shakes but would have set a peasant back a full summer's harvest.

I pulled my gear out of my pockets. The rest of the gang stood up. Several of them grunted in surprise to see that I wasn't unarmed after all.

Diccon came on. He tried to put himself in a posture of defense but he had no training. I cut at his shield low and overloaded it in a shower of sparks and a momentary blue haze. My stroke finished by severing the boy's right leg at mid-thigh.

He toppled onto his side. I leaped over his body, and laid into the rest of the gang before they realized they were in a serious battle. One I thrust through the chest before he got his shield on. A second was trying to run away when I swiped him spine-deep across the back.

I tried to get the red-haired leader but rather than face me he sprang off the node, accompanied by a brindled lurcher with a lot of collie in him. One of the remaining band made a full-armed swing at me. I took the blow on my shield without bothering to parry. His weapon came near to overloading from the stroke which the shield shrugged off untroubled.

He ran onto the Road just as his leader had, and the rest of the gang followed without hesitation. I realized I was lucky. There were still eight or nine of them and their arms, though not of top quality, would have permitted them to surround me and bring me down if they'd had time to think.

That of course was why I'd attacked the way I had, giving the gang no time to plan.

I continued to face the barrier in case some of them came back to the node to try conclusions. None of them did. I looked at the bodies I'd felled in my first rush. Baga had put a tourniquet on Diccon's leg. My chest thrust had opened the second man like a deer unlaced for the hounds which had hunted it. The man with the severed spine lay facedown as he'd fallen. His fingers opened and closed without strength and his eyes blinked as he looked at me. He didn't speak.

I was shaking with exhaustion. If any of the gang had remained in the node I would have continued killing them—living on my nerves. Now that the pressure had come off, I was a marionette whose strings had been cut. I'm not sure how I could have reacted if the guards *had* come back then.

Baga returned from the tents with a double armload of blankets. The guards had been carrying much more baggage than was normal on the Road where humans were the primary beast of burden. They'd been hired primarily as porters since Lady Irene couldn't be left to rough it. Perhaps if Lord Ercole had been choosing guards rather than menials and trusting defense to a Champion, he would have considered their character more carefully.

"What do we do now, boss?" Baga said. He looked into the pot hanging over the fire by its bail. I'd already checked to find dried meat and potatoes which had probably been carried dried also.

"We wait," I said. "According to her maid, Lady Irene regularly vanished back at Banft but she always returned. We can only hope that she does the same this time. We could search the ruins but I wouldn't expect to have better luck than the guards did earlier."

"Whatever you say, boss," Baga said. "I sure don't have a better idea."

Neither did I, but this didn't seem to me to be a very good one.

CHAPTER 3

Damsel in Distress

Baga was sleeping in one of the two tents with Diccon, who was still alive. Sam and I used the groundsheet as a low cover. He nestled his back close to me for the warmth. I felt him when he stirred and raised my head though I hadn't heard anything myself.

My eyes caught motion in the direction Sam was facing. In a low voice I said, "Lady Irene, we are friends and the guards are gone. I am Pal of Beune, one of Jon's Champions."

She'd been heading toward the cold fire, so I added, "There's food and water here."

"Look," she said in a harsh, angry voice. She was holding something in her right hand, but I didn't think it was a weapon. "I can return to the Underworld in an instant. You *can't* hold me."

"I don't want to hold you," I said. We were still speaking in low voices, but I saw the flap of Baga's tent twitch. I hoped he wouldn't come out because I believed Irene about vanishing whenever she wanted to. "I want to escort you wherever you want to go. A wounded guard told me that was Westbriggan, though I'll have to ask people along the way for directions. Unless you know all the turns yourself."

"Why are you doing this?" Irene asked. Her dim figure didn't exactly relax, but she seemed less like a frightened fawn.

I sat up, leaning so that the ground sheet didn't brush the top of my head.

"I'm a Champion," I repeated, though I wasn't sure Irene

19

knew what that entailed. "I heard that Jon had assigned another Champion, Lord Frobier, to escort you but he'd taken sick. People told me that you'd fallen into the hands of really bad men, so I followed to rescue you. You didn't need rescue, but I thought you might still need an escort. I offer myself."

"You're a friend of Frobier?" she said.

"I am not," I said. "I make the offer out of duty to the Leader Jon and to the Commonwealth itself. We Champions can't make all Mankind safe, but we make it better when we're able to. This is a case I think I can make better, if you'll let me."

Irene sighed. "If you can give me some water, that will help me for now. And after that we can discuss other matters."

I waved toward Baga's tent and called, "Bring the canteen out for the lady, Baga."

Lady Irene drank greedily. She wiped the wooden mouth of the bottle with the palm of her hand, but she didn't insist on a tumbler.

"Why do you want to go to Westbriggan?" I asked. Baga offered her one of our own sausages; the guards probably had a store of food also.

"My cousin Sarah won't force me to go to Lord Diederich," she explained. "She never liked my father and would be horrified that he sold me to Diederich—for that's what it was."

"I very much doubt that Jon would force you to go to Diederich," I said. "He can't have understood the actual situation when he directed Lord Frobier."

"Are you sure?" Irene said. "Frobier didn't seem to care what I thought."

"Lord Frobier isn't here," I said. "I'll venture to take you to Dun Add and stand as your Champion before Jon if that's even necessary."

"You will?" she said. "Why would you do that?"

I smiled. "Because it's my duty," I said, "and I believe in justice. Understand, that's assuming that the facts are as you say. If they aren't, you're on your own, so make up your mind to tell the truth—or else go to Westbriggan if your cousin doesn't care about the truth."

"If you'll stand by me with the Leader," Lady Irene said, "I'd much prefer to go to Dun Add."

"Then that's what we'll do," I said. I looked around. It was close enough to dawn that the sky was noticeably bright in the East. Lady Irene for the first time noticed the two bodies who lay where they'd fallen Baga, and I had no tools with which to bury them, even in loose sand. I suppose we could have scooped with our bare hands but I didn't feel like doing that—nor ordering Baga to.

"What happened to them?" Irene asked.

"They attacked me," I said. "There's a wounded one in Baga's tent that I guess I'll send folks from Boyd back to get. If he's still alive."

"I see," said Irene. Then she said, "Do we have to go back to Boyd?"

I thought for a moment. "No," I said. "We can turn the other way when we leave here. If you'd like, we'll do that."

I wasn't afraid of Lord Frobier, especially given how sick he'd been when I'd last seen him. I was just as glad to avoid a nasty interview, though. "Do you need to sleep before we set off then?"

"No," Irene said. "I'm ready to leave right now."

Baga and I were travelling light, and we hadn't really unpacked anyway, so it was only a minute or two before I could help him shrug the pack onto his back. We were all—Sam included—glad to get away from this nameless node. I would ask somebody to go back for Diccon, but if no one at the next node was interested in doing so, I wasn't going to lose sleep. I'd been *trying* to kill the boy, after all, to save our own lives.

"Ma'am?" Baga said. "Your ladyship, I guess. Since we're all friends now... Where in heaven is it that you go off to when you disappear?"

I wasn't certain we were all friends, at least in Irene's mind, but it was a question I'd been wondering about too.

"I was raised by a Maker named Master Sans," she said after a moment. She gestured with the bundle of yarrow stalks she was carrying in her right hand. "He'd found or maybe made a place that isn't really part of Here. He could get into it by going into a Maker's trance but it took time and concentration. Have you ever seen a Maker working?"

"I'm a Maker myself," I said. I knew exactly how much effort was required.

"Well, Sans wanted a quicker process and he thought he could turn me into a key with some tools the Ancients had left in the place he'd found," Irene said. "Sans called it the Underworld, so I do too. I don't need these—" She waggled the yarrow stalks "—but they make it quicker for me to open the passage than it would be without throwing them. A crutch, if you will. Do you male Makers use them too?"

"A few do, yes," I said. "There's one of the weaponsmiths in Master Louis's shop who always looks into a kaleidoscope before he starts work. But ma'am—from what you said, do you think of yourself as a Maker yourself?"

"Of course I do," she said. "Of course I *am*. I go into a trance and adjust atoms to create devices the way the Ancients did. What would you call it?"

I thought about it. "I've never known a female Maker," I said. "And with men we're moving actual atoms. But that isn't what you're doing, is it? I mean you're not making things the way I do? Not that I could see afterward when I looked after you reappeared."

Irene looked increasingly angry. "So," she said. "You couldn't see it so I didn't really open a way from Here to the Underworld? I suppose I didn't vanish either?"

"Ma'am," I said, "I'm just trying to understand. You surely vanished, but I don't see how from looking where you were afterward."

"Then I suppose the pattern in the air atoms reformed after it opened a path for me," she said. "Do you expect me to know what happens after I've left?"

"No ma'am," I said, trying to sound reasonable. "I was just trying to understand."

After a moment I cleared my throat and added, "Ma'am, is this something I could learn to do?"

"Master Sans taught himself to enter the Underworld on his own," Irene said. "He found the tools he used to train me in the Underworld so he didn't have the use of them yet. I suppose you could do the same thing."

"But if I did use the training devices?" I said.

Irene paused on the Road and looked hard at me. "If I were to give you access to the tools," she said, "I suppose it would be easier than it would without the training. I will tell you, though, that Master Sans used the tools frequently but he never became as skilled as I am in going between Here and the Underworld. He decided that women's minds were better for the purpose."

I said, "Thank you. I like to understand things, and I thought that might make it easier for me to do that."

I regretted the defensive tone in everything Irene said to me, but she'd replied and I could be polite. As Clara had said, Irene had had a strange upbringing. I didn't imagine either her father or Master Sans were good introductions to men.

"Your father's still alive, I gather," I said. "What of Master Sans, though?"

"He had a crystal pavilion in the Underworld where he worked," she said, "but there was a great park around it with a herd of deer. I don't know if he stocked the park itself or found them there the way he found everything else. He made sex dolls for my father from newborn fawns. They didn't live very long, but when one died I was sent down to escort a new one up to my father. When I went down most recently, I found that a monster had entered the park. From the Waste, I suppose."

She took a deep breath and went on, "Sans wasn't in the pavilion when I entered, I always entered there. I went out into the compound and the deer were gone but I found hooves and lower legs. The ends were ragged, bitten off. I didn't see Master Sans, but the thing came out of the Waste and chased me back to the pavilion and it almost got me. It was a mouse—only it was huge and it had a really long snout and it wriggled through the doorway at me but it couldn't quite reach. It was *awful.*"

I'd seen beasts from the Waste. There can't have been many of them, though I'd seen two. The first was home on Beune when I was a kid, I guess a slug if it hadn't been so huge and eating a farmer's field down to the bedrock.

I got credit with the neighbors for driving it back into the Waste with a weapon I made myself from a rock drill and took seven minutes to recharge. All I credit myself with is standing there when the thing came toward me. I deserve credit for courage—and maybe for luck, that the thing had decided to wander off after I'd pricked it but probably for no reason to do with me.

The other was something that looked like a dragon and I suppose was, flying to a node that wasn't on the Road and happened to be where a villain with a boat had marooned a girl. That one I truly had driven off. I figured I could do the same for this mouse that Irene had seen—if I ever needed to.

"I went back to Banft without a doll," Irene concluded. "My

father was furious. The envoys who'd come from Lord Diederich were still there and father accepted Diederich's offer for me."

"That's awful," I said. There are plenty of bad parents, in Dun Add as surely as there had been on Beune, but I'd never heard of anything as brutally callous as what Irene had just described.

"I suppose it is," she said. "Going to Dun Add seemed a better choice than going to Lord Diederich or returning home until my father found another buyer for me."

"That isn't right," I said.

I couldn't speak for the Commonwealth, but I could sure speak to Jon. I didn't think I'd need to be very forceful with Jon, though I was certainly willing to be. Actually where my mind was leaning was to carry Irene back to Banft and put my opinion of Lord Ercole's behavior to him directly. The purpose of the Commonwealth was to replace feud and private murder with a system of courts and trials. To give in to my personal will would subvert the system I was sworn to uphold. I wasn't going to do that.

Sam noted the flaw in the Waste that marked the entrance and turned toward it before I directed him. I hoped there was a proper inn where we were stopping. I'm perfectly willing to doss down on an uninhabited node, but yesterday and last night hadn't been very restful.

The inn was right on the edge of landingplace. Mostly they were set back deeper in the node because until recently some of the travellers down the Road weren't folks you really wanted to meet. This inn's location was a real pat on the Commonwealth's back.

There was a stable for dogs to the right of the two-story frame building. The casement windows in front had lace curtains; I could see movement behind them.

"Take care of Sam, Baga," I said. "I wouldn't be surprised if they stocked wine instead of beer here."

I'm a lager drinker for choice, but Baga preferred wine and tonight I didn't mind him really tying one on. He'd been a good servant to me.

Lady Irene stepped onto the porch with me. I opened the front door and gestured the lady in before me and followed. "Can you find us two separate rooms, innkeeper?" I called to the figure behind the counter as my eyes adjusted.

"We'll find you something," said a voice from behind us. I turned and caught a glimpse of the red-haired Errol just as he switched on his weapon and his figure blurred. The men deeper in that inn were Lady Irene's guards also, bringing their weapons live on all sides.

I'd had it. I'd screwed up and we were doomed as a result. I grabbed for my shield and weapon, but they were on all sides.

Irene shouted, "Lord Pal!" and flung something at the floor. Reality shattered.

Lady Irene leaped through the hole and I followed her.

I sprawled on a hard floor. Irene was just in front of me, picking up her scattered yarrow stalks. I turned quickly and switched on my equipment. None of the guards had followed us.

Baga and Sam were outside or already in the stables. I hoped they'd be all right. Obviously I had my own problems but their situation worried me more: they were in a pickle because of me. I'd made my own decisions—and besides, at bottom I always believed I could get myself out of any situation I got into.

We were in a high-roofed room with crystalline walls. I would have to go into a trance to check the crystalline structure but from other Ancient sites I was sure the walls were diamond. There were boxes and crates along the walls and in a corner was a fountain over a basin. I recognized that as a device which converted any sort of organic matter into food and potable water. Ancient boats like mine used similar ones to feed the boatman and passengers, and Guntram had refurbished a small one to provision him on the rare occasions he travelled by the Road.

"What is this place?" I asked Irene. The boxes contained rods of varied materials. They had no meaning for me, but along the wall opposite the single narrow doorway was a narrow container which might be a coffin. It was plumbed for fluids.

"This was Master Sans workroom," she said. "This is where I go when I flee Here and where Master Sans raised me."

I gestured to the coffin-like container. "This is where Sans made the dolls for your father?" I asked.

"Yes," Irene said. She grimaced, then looked directly at me and said, "I will not be a sexual partner for you, Lord Pal."

She kept her voice calm, but I could feel fury not far beneath the surface.

"Ma'am, Lady May and me, she's one of the Consort's ladies in waiting, are a couple. I had no intention of insulting you by my attentions."

She looked as though she was poised to claw my eyes out, despite my reassuring words. At least I meant them to be.

In our short acquaintance I'd given her no reason to doubt my good intentions. It might be that Lord Frobier had—but surely I deserved to be judged by my own behavior. Not for the first time I realized that the world wasn't fair. I suspected Lady Irene would have agreed with that, but she would have spun it in a different direction.

I walked to the single doorway through the crystal walls. It was only about two feet wide—a tight squeeze, even for me. Beyond was a park of deciduous trees with eight-inch-diameter trunks. There was a scattering of oak leaves and acorns on the ground but it was too sparse to completely cover the roots. There were even patches of grass.

I turned back to Irene. "How far does this go?" I asked. "The grounds, I mean."

"There's a boundary about half a mile from the pavilion," she said. "If you walk through it, you turn around and find yourself walking back. The same thing happens to deer. I've watched them."

That didn't make much sense to me. I said, "I'm going to look for myself," and started off across the park. There were no points of reference in this compound. The trees were roughly the same size and species (oaks); on the other hand prospecting in the Waste had polished my sense of direction.

"But wait!" Irene called. I turned. "You're forgetting the monster, the giant mouse."

"I need to deal with it sometime if we stay here," I said. "I'd sooner have it over and done with."

I knew that mice—or any rodent—could give a hell of a bite. But I didn't see them going on a killing spree that left severed legs and hooves strinkled across the compound—as I could see for myself this one had done. I wondered how many deer there'd been in Master Sans's herd before the monster had gnawed his way through it?

"Lord Pal," Irene called, "don't leave me. I don't want to be alone."

I looked back at her, standing in the doorway. "The only way you can be safe is to stay where you are. But if you insist on being with me, come along. We're going to walk to this barrier."

After an instant's hesitation, she darted out to join me. I didn't want her with me when we were likely to be attacked from any direction, but it struck me that she could return to Here any time she wanted to. If I told her she was on her own, I might very well find her gone when I returned to the pavilion.

"What happens if we return to Here when we reach the barrier?" I asked. "Are we half a mile from the inn? Or do we take a chance of winding up in the Waste?"

"We go back to exactly where we were when we entered the Underworld," she said. "The same when I enter the Underworld: it's always in the pavilion."

The thing came out of the Waste behind us—between us and the pavilion. I smelled its arrival rather than hearing it. It wasn't a long-snouted mouse but rather a shrew the size of an ox. I turned to face it, bringing both shield and weapon live. Irene cried out and maybe I did too. The shrew and I rushed together. My shield would slow physical missiles shot at me but I didn't know what effect it would have on a creature that must have weighed a ton.

I aimed my weapon at the shrew's left shoulder rather than at the wriggling snout. The blade cut in, adding the stench of burning hair to that of the shrew's musk. The beast twisted its long jaws to clamp on me, but because of my shield the movement bunted me out of the way.

I didn't lose my footing but I fetched up against a tree hard enough to stun me. The shrew shrieked and lunged at me again. I wasn't able to pick a target this time but slashed across the thing's muzzle. It turned and I charged, cutting deep above the short tail. I couldn't afford to let it get away, because it could come back through the Waste.

The shrew began to thrash. Its hind legs didn't work anymore. When it twisted at me again, I thrust through the low skull, hearing the creature's skull crackle and seethe.

I backed away from the dying creature. Only then did I think of Irene. I turned and said to her I was afraid we'd smashed into her in the fight. "You're all right then?"

Her eyes didn't seem to focus. "How did you do that?" she said.

"I said I'd deal with it!" I snapped. I really didn't want to think about what had just happened. "If you're all right, we'll go on."

"Are you angry?" Irene said. "I don't know why you should be."

I resumed walking on. I'd been scared to death and I *didn't* want to talk about it. I suppose I could've said that, but I really didn't want to talk about it.

Irene followed me. I was in a bad mood, which wasn't fair. But surely I wasn't the only man who didn't want to yammer when he thinks he's on the edge of losing it. If I could just keep moving on, I'd be fine.

I'd switched off and thought about putting my gear back in my pockets, but I wasn't sure the shrew was alone. "I think we're close to the barrier," Irene said though the woods ahead of us looked the same to me. "Here!"

I paused, then shuffled forward. I still couldn't feel anything but my leading foot began to vanish as though it had been cut off at mid-instep. I didn't feel anything. There was motion on the ground near where my foot was disappearing. My foot was reappearing beside itself. I recognized the rough-out leather that Herman, the best cobbler on Beune, had used for the shoes, but to be sure I waggled the toes. I couldn't imagine how that was happening.

My left hand with the shield went through and reappeared beside itself also. I took a deep breath and switched on my weapon to be ready for whatever was on the other side and jumped fully through the barrier.

Being on the different plane that the weapon put me into made no difference. I stepped out beside where I had entered the barrier, but now facing in toward the pavilion.

I switched off my weapon again and saw Lady Irene staring at me in obvious amusement. "Now that you've proved I was telling the truth," she said, "what do you propose to do?"

"What happens if you treat this barrier as you would the interface between the Underworld and Here?" I said. "Where do you wind up then?"

"I don't know," she said. "I didn't think of that."

She stared hard at either a distant tree or something I couldn't see. She cast her yarrow stalks on the ground beside me. The air separated, not shattering as it had done a moment ago in Here but rather the way frost vanished from a sunstruck window pane. I stepped into the room beyond.

CHAPTER 4

Neighbors

I didn't feel anything when I walked through the barrier, any more than I had when it was turning my attempts backward. I was in a room that was empty except for a chair fixed in the middle facing one wall. I'd apparently entered through the back of the room; there was an ordinary doorway in the wall to the right.

I turned to see Irene entering through the melted hole as I had and kneeling to pick up her yarrow stalks again. I guess they were the thing she counted on to keep her safe from sudden attacks—the way I did my weapon and shield.

When it happened, Irene's bolt hole had saved us when I'd been too late in getting out my hardware. Now she looked at the wall the chair faced and said, "An image screen like the one in my compound! Show us the inn where we were ambushed."

"Do you mean me?" I said, but the wall was answering her by becoming a window onto the room we'd just escaped from in the common room that I'd barely glimpsed. Half a dozen of Irene's guards stood around Baga. They were threatening and several had their weapons out, but they weren't actually knocking him around.

Irene looked at me in puzzlement. "How did you do that?" I said, gesturing to the figures. We weren't hearing them. "Make them appear, I mean."

"I just told the screen what I wanted it to display," I said. "I assume it's Ancient work like everything in the Underworld."

The window changed without Irene directing it. A man of thirty or so was facing us. "Good day," he said. "I am Blessus and you are very welcome in this place. I took this method of greeting you lest you react as though I were an enemy, which I surely am not."

"What is this place?" I asked. I probably sounded harsher than I meant to be. I was surprised and I suppose frightened.

"We are in an enclave in the Waste," Blessus said. "I believe you are both from Here."

"Were you a friend of Master Sans?" Lady Irene said sharply. "We came from his compound, which is now mine."

"I have never left this enclave," Blessus said. "There are wonderful things here which you do not have in Here. Ancient artifacts as they were left in working order and others that I have repaired."

"I'd like to see that," I said. "See them."

I didn't ask Irene what she wanted because this was a wonderful opportunity for me and I had *some* rights in the matter. I only regretted that my friend Master Guntram wasn't here to share the experience.

The image of Blessus disappeared, and an instant later the man himself walked through the doorway on the right side of the room. He held what I took for a weapon loosely in his right hand. I didn't see a shield, however.

"I just wanted to make sure you knew I wasn't a threat," he said and quirked a smile at me. "Would you like to see something else on the display before we leave this room?"

"Yeah," I said. "Do I just speak the way Irene did?"

Blessus nodded, and I said, "I'd like to see Beune, Master Demetri's farm."

I guess I said that because I was missing home so much. Not the place but rather me being in the place and I guess being young. I wasn't but twenty-two now, but the past two years had been hard ones. My life had changed more than it had for all the time I'd lived in Beune with Mom and on my own after she'd died. I couldn't go back and I didn't even want to: I had everything I'd dreamed of as a kid—and a lot more.

I not only sat in Jon's Hall of Champions, I was one of the most respected members of it. I'd been a self-taught Maker, but by meeting and working with Master Guntram I'd learned more

even than I had as a warrior compared to the boy who came
to Dun Add.

There *were* no women in Beune who were even a patch on
Lady May. I'd gained her by being myself.

As I thought that, I heard from the other room Irene saying,
"Show me Lady May in Dun Add."

Instead of speaking to Blessus as my lips had been pursing
to do, I ducked back to the display. May sat on a hassock in
the Consort's suite in the palace with several other of the ladies
in waiting. Two of the Champions were socializing also, Lord
Bryson and Lord Clain. Clain when not working—he was the
Chancellor and a very good one—could generally be found in
the Consort's company.

May was holding the long-necked lute she frequently played,
though at the moment she was chatting with Clain. I pointed
her out to Irene and said, "That's May. And that's the Chancellor, Lord Clain." Then I said, "Why are you watching her? You
don't know her."

"You mentioned her and I was curious," Irene said in a cool
voice. "She has lovely long hair."

"Yes," I said. "Now, shut it off. You've satisfied your curiosity.
She doesn't deserve to be spied on. Nobody does."

"Close the display," Irene said obediently. I'd expected an
argument and didn't have any idea about what I could do to
compel her.

I returned to Blessus. I indicated the narrow tank with my
toe and said, "Do you make humanoid dolls, Master Blessus?"

I felt Irene stiffen beside me. "No," Blessus said. "The tank
was part of the compound's original fittings but I repaired it
myself. I find it relaxes me. I'm the only one who's been in the
tank since I found it."

Blessus looked completely human but so had Lang, whom I
had met beyond the Marches at the edge of the Commonwealth.
Lang had been a thing of the Waste as surely as the Wraith I'd
killed on my first journey back from Dun Add to Beune—with
my tail between my legs, I don't mind saying.

The Wraith had been the enemy of all life. So I think was
Lang. I certainly didn't trust Blessus.

Lady Irene joined us in the outer room. She looked at the
paraphernalia as I had but with greater understanding. She

removed a flexible sheet rolled tightly from a cabinet and shook it open, then laid it in the tub I'd noticed.

"This is a jig," she said to Blessus in an accusing voice. "A template. You said that you don't make dolls."

"No one has used the tank but myself," Blessus said. "What you see are things that the Ancients left, for whatever reason they left them."

I don't know if Irene believed him or not, but I did. It left other questions, though.

There was movement outside among the trees of the compound. My frozen attention drew the eyes of the other two.

"It's another shrew!" I said, taking my equipment out again. "Go back to the inner room. It can't fit through the doors. I'll take care of it."

"There's no need of that," Blessus said. "I will kill it."

He hefted his weapon, taking it in both hands. I got a good look at it for the first time. Instead of a tube, it was three four-inch tubes spaced equidistant around one that was about ten inches long. I would have to spend considerable time with it in a trance to see how the assemblage was interconnected. I was pretty sure even with a cursory scan that though parts of it were Ancient work at least some was recent.

Blessus stepped out into the compound. The shrew sensed him—I wasn't sure how good its sight was—and came toward us with a fast sinuous motion around the trees. I thought of a creek moving swiftly over the rocks of a steep streambed.

Blessus held out the weapon. There was a dazzling flash like a lightning bolt from the end of the weapon to a sapling twenty feet from where Blessus stood. The sapling—I think it was a dogwood—exploded into a red torch just in front of the shrew.

It jumped into the air with an earsplitting screech and stood upright for an instant before springing again toward Blessus. He shouted also and ducked around the pillar he'd been standing in front of.

With my shield advanced, I went out to face the monster as I'd intended to do in the first place. The fur of the shrew's muzzle and chest was singed. It was insane with rage, though the term may not be applicable to a creature with no waking thought but to kill.

I thrust into the lower jaw. My point glanced from the row

of teeth but dug into edge of the lip with a sizzle and hiss. The shrew sprang backward as though it were a bent tree limb.

"Pal, come back!" Lady Irene said.

I charged the shrew, striking for the muzzle again. The beast was too angry to be afraid of pain. It snapped at me, bouncing me back against a pillar; a hard knock, but I didn't hit my head. I thrust at its left eye and the point bit deeper than it had on tooth enamel.

The shrew kept worrying my shield, jerking his head back and forth and pulling me with it. I didn't let go of it, though, so the long jaws were never able to close on me. I continued to cut at the monster's skull. Every time it tossed its head, blood spattered me.

The shrew suddenly collapsed. I jerked away and found I could barely stand. The shrew's squeals and yips must have been deafening for when they stopped my ears were numb.

I sat down heavily on the diamond floor of the building. "When my weapon recharged, I wasn't able to use it again because you and the creature were so close together," Blessus said.

"We got the job done without it," I said.

"But it would've been so much easier—" he began.

"It would've been a hell of a lot easier if you hadn't stirred it up with your toy!" I shouted. If I hadn't been so tired I would've kept my temper.

"Well regardless, it's done," Blessus said.

Irene hadn't moved from where she was when the shrew attacked. She said to me, "You could have been killed."

"I'm a Champion," I said. "This is the job. I knew that when I came to Dun Add."

After a moment I said, "What I'd like now is a meal. Does this site have that available, Master Blessus?"

"At very high quality," Blessus said and led us into another inner room in which banquette seating surrounded a table on which a flat disk sat and dispensed whatever dish we requested. I asked for roast goose. The result was very like the best I'd eaten on Beune. The texture was odd, but it was more tender than Mother Hollert's geese ever had been in my recollection. Lady Irene seemed happy with her fruit selection, while Blessus himself was eating some sort of flat bread. I hadn't heard what he'd called it.

"This is very good," I said, wiping my hands on a piece of toweling beside my place. I turned to Lady Irene and said, "Are you ready to move on, milady? Do you think we'll be back in the inn again where we were ambushed if we start from here?"

"I have no idea," Irene said. "I suppose so. What will happen then?"

I thought about it and said, "I guess I'll see what I can do to your gang of guards if they don't have the drop on me. I figure if you can keep giving me a way out, I can keep whittling the numbers down two or three at a time until they're all dead."

"That sounds horrible!" Irene said.

I shrugged. "I don't like the idea either, but I need to rescue Baga and Sam," I said. "I figure being able to watch the guards before I attack I can get Errol right at the start and I think the rest of them will leave us alone."

"Lord Pal and Lady Irene," Blessus said. "You don't have to leave at all, you realize. You're welcome to stay as long as you wish. Your presence is a great pleasure to me."

"Thank you, Master Blessus," I said, "but I have job to do back in Here. And I have people I want to get back to." May and others, but especially May.

I decided to take a chance, though. "Blessus, you're a very skilled Maker," I said. "If you'd like to come to Dun Add, I can introduce you to people almost as skilled as you are."

"If I were to leave," Blessus said, "I would have to leave all this—the devices could not be transported. And you have nothing comparable in Dun Add, I have watched you."

"But perhaps you and Master Guntram working together might advance Dun Add," I said. And that was true—but not in any real sense. The Underworld contained surviving Ancient artifacts to a degree no part of Here did. It wasn't just knowledge that Blessus would have to leave here but a huge quantity of physical artifacts that all the Makers in Dun Add couldn't duplicate in a century.

"No, no," Blessus said. "But there's no need to decide immediately."

Lady Irene stood up. "Master Blessus?" she said. "Would you direct me to the bath in your compound? If you don't have one I'll have to go back to my own. And Lord Pal, will you be ready to resume our journey in the morning?"

"Sure," I said. I was amused at the way she had cut through our host's profitless chattering.

I got up. I was ready right now to kill Errol and as many of his henchmen as it took until the survivors decided to leave us alone. I didn't like the situation, but I hadn't created it.

"There is a bath here," Blessus said. "It may not be safe for you to leave the pavilion with two if these monsters coming from the Waste while you're here. I wonder if you're drawing them, Lady Irene?"

"I was here many times before with Master Sans," Irene said. "And I was back in Banft with my father when the first thing killed Master Sans."

"If another shrew or anything else attacks her," I said, "I'll deal with it as you've seen. Now, our quarters, please?"

"There are three suites of rooms besides the one I use myself," Blessus said. "Each contains a bath."

He led us into a narrow corridor. I wondered what this structure had been when the Ancients built it?

Blessus gestured Lady Irene to a doorway. "I wish you would rethink your determination to leave, Irene," he said. "You are reacting on a surface level but I'm sure that if you took time to consider you would find many advantages to remaining here."

"I am sure I would not!" Irene said sharply. "Master Blessus, you aren't any more human than the dolls Sans made for my father were. You have used the same tools to make yourself a close copy of a human—but you aren't one. We will leave in the morning."

"If that were true," Blessus said, "would it be so very bad? Someone whose whole being is focused on being human and has Ancient resources to achieve that. With you to help and guide him, Lady Irene, he could achieve marvelous things."

Irene shouted on a rising note, "You're not *human*! Leave me alone!"

The panel closing the doorway was too light to slam, but she shut it as hard as she could in ducking inside her suite.

Blessus sighed and said, "And what do you think, Lord Pal? Am I human?"

"I don't really know what human is," I said truthfully. "I said I would take you to Dun Add and sponsor you."

"Thank you for your honesty," he said. I wondered if he

realized I did *not* believe he was human and that I would say as much to my superiors in Dun Add. "What of Lady Irene?" Blessus asked. "Might she at some point change her mind about me and about the situation?"

"I know very little about what women think," I said truthfully. But because I was so tired, I didn't leave it there and instead continued, "I very much doubt that Irene will change her mind. She has fixed opinions about men and I doubt she ever changes them."

"I see," said Blessus. "Again, thank you for honesty."

He opened the door of the suite beyond Irene's. I collapsed on the raised sleeping platform, not even bothering first to bathe. I was exhausted from fighting the second shrew and puzzled about why I had done that when remaining in the pavilion would have been safe.

Killing the beast had been unnecessary. Perhaps I had been proving something—I suppose to myself.

CHAPTER 5

Dealing with Things

In the night I heard a scream. I hadn't undressed, so drawing my shield and weapon were second nature. The only difficulty was the tangle of bedding around my legs.

I stumbled into the corridor. Against the light in the banqueting room beyond I saw Blessus carrying Irene over his shoulder. He pressed his own weapon against her as she struggled against him.

"Help me, Pal," she shouted.

"I'll deal with it," I said.

"If you come closer I will shoot you!" Blessus said.

My shield jarred me as I started to charge through the narrow doorway. I dropped it and went on with my weapon in front of me.

"Don't!" Blessus shouted.

I rushed him. He was trying to point his clumsy weapon at me but the bolt glanced off the diamond wall to my left. It felt as though I'd brushed glowing iron.

His weapon was harmless for the moment but I cut down at it to finish the business. It wrecked itself in sparks and crackling.

Lady Irene wrenched herself away. "Kill him!" she shouted. "Kill him!"

I was breathing hard. My weapon was still live. "No," I said. "Not unless I already have."

I'd cut as carefully as haste allowed—not because I cared

about Blessus, but he and Lady Irene were tangled. I'd gotten at least some of his fingers when I sheared through the body of his weapon and it looked like I'd cut his cheek also. He was surely a bloody mess despite the cauterizing effect of my weapon at high intensity. None of the wounds I'd inflicted looked life threatening, though.

His own weapon had exploded when I cut it though, and his abdomen was a bloody, blackened mess.

"Irene!" I said. "You know how that tank in the other room works, don't you? We'll put Blessus in that and rebuild him. He's still alive!"

"Why would we do that?" Irene said. "He deserves to die!"

"That's for the Lord to decide," I said. I scooped Blessus under the knees and shoulders and lifted him. I turned to settle him in the same direction as the tank. I was getting blood all over my clothes but that didn't matter any more than it had the times I've lent a hand to butchering a hog.

"No," Blessus said. I had to bend close to be sure he was speaking.

"The vat cannot make me human. I've proved that," he said. "Let whatever I am die and merge back with the Waste."

I hesitated. Blessus said, "Lady Irene will never be safe so long as this thing lives."

"Pal!" Irene said, "You cannot do that to me!"

She was right, of course. I sighed and carefully lay Blessus down on the diamond floor. I stepped away and said to him, "I don't believe you, but I can't take a chance."

"No, you can't take a chance," Blessus repeated. He began to laugh, making the blood bubble from the holes in his torn chest. He was still laughing when he finished dying.

"I really wanted to save him," I said to Irene. "He was trying so hard to be human."

"He disgusted me," said Irene. "He was the same as those dolls my father used."

"I know," I said. "But he was trying."

"He tried to kill you!" Irene said.

"He surely did," I agreed. "That weapon can't have been six feet from me when he sent the bolt."

Irene looked squarely at me. "You said you would take care of him," she said. "He was frightened. He'd watched you charge the shrew, and now you were coming for him. Pal, doesn't any-thing frighten you?"

"Lots of things do," I said. "But you have to do the right thing however scared you are." I picked up my shield, then returned it and the weapon to my pockets. "Now," I said, "speaking of things that scare me, let's look up Errol on your display. I need to kill him and a couple of his mates."

Baga was still at the inn where we'd been attacked but the band of guards was not. Irene located Errol somewhere on the Road. They'd apparently given up their vigil. That had saved the lives of some of them.

And perhaps saved my life as well.

CHAPTER 6

Back to Here

"Take us back to the inn, please, Lady Irene," I said. I took my gear out as Irene prepared her own. She flung her bundle of yarrow stalks and we stepped one after the other back into the inn parlor. A servant screamed and flung herself into what seemed to be a storage closet, but there was no worse result from our sudden appearance.

The guards had robbed Baga but they hadn't stolen Sam, for which I was grateful. I'd have tracked them down to get Sam back.

"Now what, boss?" Baga said.

I turned to Irene and said, "Lady Irene, do you still want to go to Dun Add?"

"Yes," she said.

I rubbed Sam behind the ears and said, "Let's go to Dun Add."

Lady Irene wasn't in shape for hiking to Dun Add, but it was the only way she was going to get there. Sam and I didn't push but neither do I find much entertainment in staring at the Waste along the side of the Road—which was the only thing to do if we didn't walk on.

I'd come to Dun Add the first time with a religious lady who'd been making a pilgrimage around sites some distance from Dun Add. I hadn't thought anything of it at the time.

Now I wondered how difficult the hiking had been for Dame Carole, who was in her fifties; thirty years older than Irene. She

41

hadn't seemed to be having much trouble. Maybe it was attitude. Dame Carole was certainly used to having her own way, but when confronted with reality, instead of whining, she just got on with it.

I hadn't liked Dame Carole, but I was coming to respect her.

"Lord Pal, we have to stop for a rest," called Lady Irene. I stopped where I was and waited for her to catch up with me. When she did, I walked along beside her.

I said, "We've got to keep moving, milady. If you'd like, I'll put an arm around your waist for a little support."

"I do not like the idea of you handling me!" Irene said. "Do you understand?"

"Yes, milady," I said and moved a little away to the side. I didn't blame her for being concerned about a man's intentions but it was very irritating. I wasn't going to molest her. She didn't know that—but we'd been together for long enough that she should have.

The Waste to the sides of the Road changed from apparent closely packed tree trunks—predominantly brown as my mind saw the Waste through Sam's eyes—to low scrub—which I saw as predominantly bluish green. None of the shapes or colors were real, but the apparent change was important: my mind was seeing a change, even though it couldn't identify the change with traditional shapes and colors.

Sam perked up noticeably. A group of travellers came out of a branch of the Road joining ours to the left. There were about twenty of the strangers all told—I took it for really three groups who'd met on the Road and came together for company and safety—though for the past few years the dangers were much reduced from what they'd been at the start of the Commonwealth.

There was nothing to be done about monsters wandering in from the Waste, but they had never been common. When a Champion met one, he dealt with it—or his replacement did.

There were still bandits but banditry on a large scale requires a base, and any node suspected of becoming a robbers' roost very quickly got a visit from a Champion of the Commonwealth. If cleaning up the problem required a unit of the regular army, it got that too. I was proud to be a Champion of the Commonwealth. My friends and neighbors on Beune were safer because of us.

The sudden dollop of traffic clogged the Road in front of us. I could easily have bulled on through them, but instead I used them as an excuse to slow our pace to theirs. Lady Irene moved back closer to me and said, "Are you from Dun Add, Lord Pal?"

It was the first thing she'd said to me during the five days we'd been on the Road that wasn't a complaint so I responded with more enthusiasm than I might otherwise have, "Not at all, ma'am. I come from Beune, which is a lot smaller than Boyd's Node and besides isn't on the way to anywhere. I'd read romances, though, and decided that the Champions of the Commonwealth were the greatest men who ever lived. I'm enough of a Maker that I made myself a weapon and shield and went off to Dun Add two years ago."

"You made your equipment?" Irene said. "I didn't know that was possible."

"I made the equipment I was using then," I corrected her. "It was junk, but it gave me enough confidence to go to Dun Add and I made friends there. I guess you could say it was all upward from then."

"And the Leader made you one of his Champions even though you're from nowhere?" Irene said. "If you don't mind me putting it that way."

"That's the truth whether I mind it or not," I said. "You earn a place in the Hall of Champions. I'll say that most Champions are better born than I am because they're more likely to have equipment of decent quality. Which I didn't have, like I tell you."

"I see," Lady Irene said. "You're telling me you're unusually skilled as a warrior, then. I knew that, I saw you fight that shrew."

"No, I wasn't saying that," I said. "Lord Clain himself couldn't have fought his way through the Aspirants' Tournament using the crap I brought to Dun Add the first time. But I made friends with the most subtle Maker in the Commonwealth, Master Guntram, and he got me the hardware I'm using now."

"I'd heard that Master Louis is the Leader Jon's chief Maker," Irene said, frowning. "He's the man whom Master Sans spoke of."

I'd forgotten that Irene had specialist knowledge of the Maker's art. I nodded to her in acknowledgment and said, "Louis is a specialist in weapons," I agreed, "and there's nobody his equal in that specialty. I think he could turn an Ancient writing stylus into a Champion-grade weapon. Right now that's what the Commonwealth needs. But nothing else interests him."

"And this Master Guntram?" Irene said.

"Everything interests Guntram," I said. "And someday the

Commonwealth may want to know how the Ancients made those displays you learned to use in the Underworld and all the other wonderful things the Ancients had that weren't weapons and shields. Guntram will be the man to show them and people with minds like him."

I cleared my throat. I had that kind of mind, but not a shadow of the skill that Guntram had.

"A thing that you said earlier that I ought to come back to," I said. "What you saw with the shrews wasn't any great skill on my part. I just went in and stabbed them to death. A joust with a Champion is a real test of skill, and there are warriors better than I am. The shrews were just dumb animals. Lots of folks could have done that."

"But would they have?" Lady Irene said.

I saw what she meant and said, "I think about any Champion would have. And ma'am, courage isn't that hard to find, not really. Skill is a different matter, but when we were out in the woods and the shrew came up behind us—what else was there to do but go for it?"

"You could have frozen and let both of us be eaten," she said.

I laughed and said, "That doesn't appeal to me." Then I said, "Lady Irene, we've reached Dun Add. I'm going to take you to a place you can stay."

We stepped through the misty boundary between the Road and the node of Dun Add, the capital of the Commonwealth. The large party we were following were mostly strangers to Dun Add and had therefore stopped as soon as they reached landingplace, blocking passage for those following them. Sam was used to such thoughtlessness and forced his way through the legs of the gawkers. I followed. Sam had shoved them at knee height; I bumped their shoulders but then pushed the plump lady on my left a little farther away so that Lady Irene could get through without contact.

The first thing to do was to get through the formalities. I headed immediately for the Herald of the Gate. I didn't push anybody out of the way, but I didn't call Sam back when he loped ahead and used his weight to get to the Herald before the visitor with a much smaller mongrel managed to do so.

The Herald looked up in irritation but then recognized me and passed the protesting stranger off to his clerk. The visitor was no worse off for the change. The Herald's clerk would run him through in a businesslike fashion without the posturing the Herald would have gone through.

I nodded politely to the Herald and said, "Baga will run through the formalities for me and Lady Irene of Banft. The Leader sent Lord Frobier to escort her, but when he fell ill I was fortunately close enough to take over."

"Of course, Lord Pal," the Herald said. While he was bowing to Lady Irene, I murmured to Baga, "After you've stabled Sam, go back to the house and tell May that I'm back but I'm stopping off with Morseth to take care of business before I come home. And I may have to check in with Clain and the Leader as well. But I'll be back as soon as I can be."

"Right," said Baga. "How many for dinner, boss? You know she'll ask."

"Right," I agreed. "Just me tonight. Irene's going to be staying with Morseth till we get her settled, okay?"

"I'll tell the Mistress," Baga said. He sounded doubtful. I didn't blame him.

There are several paths from landingplace through the band of horse chestnuts before we'd reach the base of South Street, which was paved. One of these days the pavement would probably be extended all the way to landingplace; but I, for one, would regret that. This was Dun Add as I'd come to it. I didn't want the simpler parts to change.

"How far do we have to go?" Irene asked. "I'm quite tired."

"Two blocks, is all," I said, trying to sound cheerful. Lady Irene hadn't been raised for the kind of life she'd been leading on the Road. I understood that. But you know being around somebody who's angry and resentful all the time makes the hike itself seem twice as far as it would be with somebody positive or at least neutral about the business.

"And who is this Morseth?" Irene said, making the name sound like something you'd step around on the sidewalk.

"Lord Morseth," I said, still upbeat, "is one of the most senior and respected Champions in the hall. He's also a close friend. You'll be as safe with him as you would be with me."

"I expected to be lodged in the palace," Irene said. "My father is Duke of Banft, you realize."

"I shouldn't wonder if that's what Jon decides," I said, "as soon as he realizes the situation. Remember, he arranged with your father to escort you to Lord Diederich to be married. This is all going to be a surprise."

I cleared my throat and added to her silence, "Look, Lady Irene, this is going to work out fine and if there's any problem you have my personal promise that I'll get you to Westbriggan regardless of what Jon says. But that's a long journey, and Morseth's house is just two doors down here."

I gestured down the connecting street. Irene followed me immediately. I suspected my mention of how far she would have to hike to get to Westbriggan had decided her.

Morseth's door had a big brass knocker, but his doorman saw us coming up the street and whipped the door open, shouting inside, "Lord, it's Pal, with a lady!"

Morseth was coming out of the back when we came in the front. "Good to see you, buddy," he said. "Reaves has had a bug for three days and it makes him mean as a denned bear."

"Has he tried Guntram's couch?" I asked.

"You know," he said, "I doubt he thought of that. He's not hurt, he just feels crappy and coughs a lot. You think the couch would help?"

"I'd sure try it," I said.

Master Guntram had repaired a couch that speeded the healing of injuries. It bothered him that most Champions were leery of it even after two years of use by some of the top warriors—me among them. Folks seemed to be afraid that anything that really modified the body must have other effects than helping cuts heal or bruises go away. I'd heard that it made guys impotent. That was nonsense but it wasn't the sort of thing I felt like demonstrating to my peers.

There were Champions—Morseth among them—who rather famously had a wide acquaintance among willing women. He would be a good subject to increase acceptance of Guntram's couch, but his friend Reaves was the one with the present problem.

"I'll suggest it," he said. He glanced at Lady Irene and added, "There's no problem with it, then?"

"None at all," I assured him. "I figure whatever it is that's making him sick is the same as a knife. It's hurting the body, right?"

"You think of things in a way nobody else does, Pal," Morseth said. He was so tall that at a distance you missed how extremely powerful his body was. "I'll tell Reaves—and tell him the other part is safe too."

"Master Guntram thinks of things the same way I do," I said. "Only he's better at it. You ought to listen when he tells you something."

Morseth looked at me carefully. "Pal," he said "I watched you beat Lord Baran. I wouldn't swear that I could've done that. When I see Guntram manage something like that, I'll take his word about some of his other cute toys."

I sighed. "Your choice," I said. "I didn't come to argue. I'd like a favor. I'm going to talk to Jon about lodging Irene in the palace. Until I do, could you lodge and feed her for a couple days?"

He gave me an odd look and said, "Sure. Just so I know though, have you told Lady May about this?"

I grinned. Trust Morseth to go to the heart of the matter. "It's not what you think," I said. "But no, I haven't. I've got to do that as soon as I've cleared it with Jon, and I hope to hell that she believes me."

Morseth turned to the woman who'd just joined us in the hall. "Diane," he said, "Lady Irene here is Lord Pal's friend. She'll be staying with us a few days so have a room made up on the third floor. Will you be with us for dinner, Pal?"

"No," I said. "I'll be at home." I nodded to Irene and said, "Milady, if you would go with Morseth's housekeeper—" from the look Diane had given us all during the discussion, she was more than that "—I'll discuss a few last points with my friend here."

I didn't know how Irene was going to react, but she went off politely behind Diane.

When she was safely out of earshot, I said, "Buddy, there's one thing I've got to warn you—"

"Don't say a word," said Morseth. "I don't move in on my friends' women."

"I know you don't," I agreed, "and neither does Reaves. But Reaves drinks and I suspect he's not always sure what he's doing when he's really got a load on. But the thing I've got to say is that I'm pretty sure Irene poisoned Lord Frobier because he was going to take her where she didn't want to go. I don't think Frobier's servants did, and the guards Irene's father had hired couldn't have gotten to his food. I just thought I ought to say it."

"She doesn't just poison people to pass the time, then?" Morseth said, frowning at me.

"No, she was getting Frobier out of the way," I said. "He

would've made sure she went where her father wanted—to marry Diederich of Haft."

"Not somebody I know," said Morseth. "I don't care who she marries, so I'll take a chance. Go do what you need to do—and I suggest you make seeing May high on the list."

"With luck I'll catch her with the Consort right now," I said and started back on my way to the palace. I didn't meet Baga, returning from the stables from leaving Sam. I suspected that he'd stopped off for a stoup of wine. He'd never let his drinking become a problem while he was in my service, but it was something I needed to keep an eye on.

I nodded to a few of the people I met on South Street. I didn't know any of them so well that I needed to stop and chat. I thought about my first visit to Dun Add, a peasant boy from Beune who wanted to become a Champion of Mankind and didn't have any idea of how to go about it.

By chance I met one of the Consort's ladies-in-waiting; and because she was a nice person she took pity on my ignorance and pointed me in the right directions. I knew nothing about her at the time except that she was nice and that she was the most beautiful woman I had ever met.

Both those things are still true. Her looks don't matter a lot to me—they do matter a lot to May herself. The basic niceness of her personality matters a lot. She can fly hot and does so pretty often, but probably less often than I deserve. I'm not a bad person, but May and I are about as different as two people could be; I think a lot of times she doesn't understand that I really am acting in ignorance, or that something seems reasonable to me when any reasonable person would see that it was impossible.

I've told her I'm not interested in other women. By now she's seen plenty of evidence that it's the truth, but what she would call common sense keeps getting in the way of her believing it. That's why I was a bit leery of explaining Lady Irene.

The central core of the palace is stone, but the wings added on both ends are brick and the annex on the back—the north side—is timber and holds the regiment of practice machines on which Aspirants train and which all warriors use to keep their skills current.

I knew to enter the second door from the left. The attendant inside looked up and murmured, "Lord Pal," as I trotted up the stairs to the second floor, though I didn't recollect having seen him before.

There was another attendant at the head of the stairs and a third down the corridor at the door of the Consort's suite. The last saw me coming and shouted through the grill, "Lord Pal coming." The inside attendant had unlocked the entry before I got to him.

From a distance Lady Jolene looked thirty years younger than her real age of about fifty. Even right across the room she was a beautiful woman with hair like a cloth of gold banner.

"Pal," she called graciously. "What impossible node are you back from this time?"

Lady May had come in from the roof garden when she heard me announced. She gave me a bright smile and started around the edge of the room to join me. Besides Jolene and four of her attendants, Lord Reynes, a recent Champion, was present also, sitting beside Lady Daisenna—Daisy.

"Nowhere very exciting," I said. "I met Lord Frobier on Boyd where he'd gotten sick and took over escorting Lady Irene of Banft from him. She wanted to come to Dun Add, so I'm here to check with the Leader as to where he wants her lodged. For the time being I've got her with Lord Morseth."

"We have a spare room, Pal," May said as I'd hoped she would.

"I didn't think that was a good plan," I explained. "Morseth has more room and a full-time housekeeper. You're up at the palace most days. And I wanted somebody like Morseth, because she's a pretty woman and I don't want her being pestered. She doesn't like men, from what Frobier's servants said. I don't think she was sorry that Frobier got sick, to tell the truth."

"Frobier's a pig," May muttered unexpectedly.

"I suspect Lady Irene would agree with you," I said, "though we didn't actually discuss it."

I knew that May'd had an active social life before she met me. This was one of the times that the fact cropped up in a fashion which startled me, though.

"Jolene," May said. "Can I run off early today?"

"Of course, darling," the Consort said. "Lord Pal saved me from being boiled in oil. Anything you do for him is done for me."

May stepped close and was urging us toward the door.

I remained set and said to the Consort, "Thank you, milady, but I really need to see Jon about Lady Irene, because I really didn't do what he expected. And I'd really like to check in on Master Guntram, too, and see if he's doing all right. He had a really rough trip when last he went out."

"So did you, when you brought him back!" Lady May said.

I hugged her close and said, "I'm a Champion and I'm expected to have a rough time when I go out. Guntram's an old man and a scholar. Things aren't supposed to happen to him the way they did."

I looked down at May and added, "Love, I'll be back at the house as soon as I can be."

She rose up on tiptoes and kissed me. "You wouldn't be any good to the Commonwealth if you didn't put duty first. Or to me either, because I fell in love with the man you are."

"As quick as I can," I repeated. I kissed her in front of the whole audience and broke away, going out the door.

The Leader's suite was also on the second level but around on the east wing of the palace. I followed the corridor, occasionally saying hi to someone I knew. The waiting room was as usual full of petitioners who thought they would do better at a private hearing from Jon than by appearing in open court where matters were referred as a matter of routine to the bureaucrat into whose realm it fell.

The clerk of appearances greeted me cheerfully but said, "He'll be in court till five today, Lord Pal. If you come back after that, I'll run you right in to see him."

"Thanks, Taggert," I said. All the petitioners within earshot were staring at me as though they wished they could strike me dead. That was all right: I was seeing Jon on Jon's business. They were here on their own. "I need to see Master Guntram. So I'll come back later."

Guntram's workroom was a large space on the third level back. I was about the only person besides Guntram who regularly went there. Ordinary people tend to be afraid of Makers. Guntram played on this to safeguard his privacy (because he didn't keep a servant). On the door where a knocker would ordinarily be mounted was an Ancient artifact that looked like the tail of a lizard.

If you twisted the lizard's tail, the head appeared to stick through the panel and a voice inside the room announced you in a voice loud enough to be heard in the hall. In my case the lizard announced, "It's Lord Pal, master!" in what seemed a cheerful though raspy voice. I've heard it call, "Some twit of a servant," though. For the most part, Guntram had the privacy he desired.

I heard Guntram's shuffling footsteps for some while before the panel opened. I thought again of suggesting he get a servant to handle the menial tasks like this, but he really didn't want anybody—any layman—around when he was working.

I'd taught myself to be a Maker at home. Mom tried not to disturb me, but a peasant boy doesn't dictate the rules to the adults around him. If somebody needed help tying sheaves—or later plowing, shingling, or the like—they broke in on my trance without hesitation. I got used to it.

"I've got a little while before Jon is free," I said. "I thought I'd see whether you'd recovered."

"Well, you know I wasn't really injured," Guntram said as we walked over to his work area. "I was just weak from not moving for months."

The big room was so littered with artifacts, books, and boxes of raw materials—and goodness knew what all else—that it was difficult to navigate. The furniture was sparse and generally piled with more paraphernalia.

"The thing that distresses me is that I still don't feel like doing anything," he added. "Of course, there's nothing I *need* to do. I guess that's really the problem. I'm trying to work on some of the artifacts I've gathered over the years, but I can't convince myself that anybody cares."

"*I* care, Guntram," I said. "Your skill is an inspiration to me."

He gave me a tired smile.

I thought of Blessus. I wished even more strongly that I'd convinced him to come back. At the time I'd been thinking that Guntram would help me learn about Blessus. Now I realized that the puzzle of Blessus would have been just what Guntram needed to get back on an even keel himself.

Blessus had simply given up because he realized he would never have the thing he most wanted. Guntram instead had found that he wanted *nothing*.

"Look," I said. "What would you like me to do? There must be something I can do."

Guntram laughed, the most positive response I'd had since I came to his suite. What he said though was, "You've discovered a new law of the universe, then, Lord Pal? Your good will isn't in doubt, but I'm afraid the problem is in me and you can't change it. Nor can I, I'm afraid."

I thought of suggesting that we work on something together as we'd done a number of times in the past. Particularly in putting the boat I'd captured from villains back in the condition it was in immediately after the Ancients had built it.

Boats were self-repairing, so they survived in much better shape than other Ancient artifacts. But they needed raw materials to repair themselves and most boatmen, even those like Baga, didn't know how to access the menu in the boat. They were left guessing at needs, and mostly guessed wrong—or didn't provide specialized trace elements. The boatmen weren't Makers and weren't used to the details of elementary composition.

It struck me that if Guntram and I worked a project together again, it might help get him back into the world. I was about to suggest that when I glanced at an outside window on the west end of the room. From the sun's height I realized that I had less than an hour before Jon would be free to meet me. I had a duty to Guntram: he had been my friend and my savior.

But I had a duty to Jon also—and to May. I'd promised her that I'd be home as soon as I'd reported to Jon—and that meant I had to get there. If we went deep into trances on a workpiece complex enough to really get Guntram involved, the likelihood was that we'd still be working at midnight.

Instead of enticing Guntram to work, I told him about meeting Irene and through her of meeting Blessus.

"I've heard of Master Sans," Guntram said. "I've never met him, but I've seen some examples of what I was told was his work. Very skilled, from what I saw."

"I don't doubt that," I said, "but he doesn't appear to have been a pleasant man. From the evidence, he's dead now having been eaten by a creature from the Waste. There were many Ancient artifacts in the place that Sans worked. Perhaps Irene would take us back there so that you could see for yourself. For that matter, I'd like you to meet Irene. She doesn't have a winning personality, but she really is a Maker in her own way."

"I've always suspected the Ancients had female Makers as well as men," Guntram said. "There are artifacts which I simply can't get into. When I try, it's like watching raindrops splash off a roof slate."

For a moment I thought the old curiosity and animation were

back in my friend, but the enthusiasm died away immediately. Maybe if I got him and Irene actually together...?

"I need to go see Jon right now," I said, "but I'll be back tomorrow. Stick with us, buddy. I didn't know what to do when you disappeared, you know."

We shook hands like the friends we were, but I left afraid I was losing him, as surely as if I hadn't been able to get him out of the trap he'd gotten into. I'd seen Horsley die after he'd lost his foot in a woodchopping accident back home. Old Frances had tied off the blood vessels with fish line right away—it wasn't that. But Horsley shivered on a hot summer day until he just shut down. I got the same feeling about Guntram now.

I got back to the Leader's waiting room a little later than I'd expected. When Taggert saw me he called, "Lord Pal! The Leader came in and asked me to bring you to him as soon as you arrived. He's with delegates from the timber industry now but I'm sure he'd want me to alert him."

I shrugged but followed Taggert to the door past people waiting on benches. Being run in this way sounded like a new job rather than anything to do with my report. Not that timber merchants were likely to be of critical importance to the Commonwealth.

Taggert tapped on the door, then opened it and stuck his head in. "Lord Pal is here," he said. Jon came immediately to the door and then said over his shoulder to men still within the room, "Gentlemen, I'm very sorry, but I must deal with an important matter that just came to light! Lord Pal, please come with me."

"Yes, my lord," I said, wishing I knew more about the business than that the Leader wanted to get out of a boring meeting.

We turned left down a short corridor to a meeting room Jon used to keep groups separate. He murmured to me, "A Maker kidnapped his bride twenty-five years ago. He's Count of Midian and he says he'll join the Commonwealth if we get her back. His Maker, Master Beddoes, hasn't been able to."

Jon tapped on the door to alert those inside and entered ahead of me.

"Count Stokes," he said immediately to the pair of men turning to face us. "This is Lord Pal, who has been able to think himself into a number of situations and I hope may have a useful viewpoint. Please explain the situation just as you did to me."

"If you think so, Lord Jon," the Count said. He was a tall man in his forties whose hair was already thinning. "Lady Marlene was a famous beauty and was courted by me and many others, including a Master Harvey, a Maker of some fame. Her father, a landowner on Midian, chose me rather than the commoner, of course.

"The day we were married Master Harvey cast the whole party into blackness and stole Lady Marlene away. He took her to a compound on the edge of landingplace. The walls are opaque except for about twenty feet of the front, which are clear."

"We could see Marlene, and she apparently could see us," Beddoes said, "but we couldn't hear her. Harvey was in the sealed-off place with her but nobody else could get in. There was nothing anyone could do."

"Was the container alive?" I asked, thinking of the cysts Guntram and I had found and gotten out of with difficulty.

"It was not," said Beddoes. "There was nothing there to get hold of. *Nothing.*"

I looked at Jon and said, "Sir, I'd like to have Guntram look at this."

"Who is Guntram?" said Stokes to me.

"He's a Maker," I said without adding superlatives. "He's my friend and has a broader range of knowledge and interests than most people."

"If a Maker were what was required," Beddoes said, "Lady Marlene would have been free years ago, wouldn't she, Lord Stokes?"

"Certainly I immediately sought out the best Makers for the problem," Stokes said. "None of them solved it."

"You see," Beddoes said, "this Harvey is using an Ancient device as the basis of his trap. If a modern Maker could solve the problem, I would have done so."

"Nevertheless, I'd like Master Guntram to take a look at the situation," I said. "I think this is the best help for a solution short of contacting Master Harvey and convincing him to change sides."

"If I see the man, I'll kill him!" Stokes snarled. "He raped my wife in front of me in his enclosure!"

"In that case," I said as calmly as I could, "then I particularly want Guntram to look at the situation."

"I'd want you to escort him, Pal," the Leader said. "We can't send Guntram out alone."

"Of course," I said. "And we'll take my boat."

The Leader had a boat of his own, but it wasn't in nearly as good condition as the one Guntram and I had spent weeks bringing back to original specification. My own boat had requested that I not do the same for the rival vessel and I hadn't volunteered the service. I suppose it was doubtful morality to do a favor to a machine rather than for the ruler of the Commonwealth, but I figured it didn't really matter to Jon so long as I loaned my boat whenever he asked.

It *did* matter to the boat. And if you don't believe machines can have personalities, you haven't been as close to them as I have.

Stokes and Beddoes were talking together, but neither Jon nor I paid attention.

"When will you go off?" Jon asked.

"Maybe tomorrow after May and I have talked," I said. "I don't plan to give Guntram much time to think about it. He's lost interest in things in a way I don't like to see."

Jon and I shook hands. Then I nodded to Stokes and said, "Be ready to leave tomorrow, probably around noon. I have a boat, so you can spare your legs."

Beddoes started asking questions, which I ignored. Lord Stokes just seemed pleased that he'd be riding.

I headed out of the palace and toward May.

Dom, the manservant May had decided that my status required, was waiting on the front step as I came down South Street. Instead of holding the door for me he ducked back inside and May herself met me at the door with a kiss.

That was a delight, but over her shoulder I saw her cousin Lord Osbourn. Since Osbourn shaped up and applied himself, he'd become a Champion three months ago. We got along fine now—but I hadn't been looking for company tonight.

"Darling," May said. "Osbourn's back from his own official mission and I invited him to dinner with us. He has some business to take care of for the next hour, though, so he's just going out now. Let's go up to discuss our own business in private until then. If that suits you?"

"It suits me right down to the ground," I said. We skipped up the stairs to the bedroom. I suppose I shouldn't have been embarrassed—May certainly wasn't.

Right now I didn't care. I'd been out a long time.

✦   ✦   ✦

The cook, Fritz, was delighted to have a guest to cook for—one who would appreciate his skill better than I did. I like good food just fine, but I'm not used to it to the point that I could say the sorts of things Fritz wants to hear. "I really liked dinner," rather than comments on the subtleties of the seasoning, is as far as I go. My mom was a terrible cook.

Well, my stepmom. My real mother lived with a monster from the Waste and had nothing to eat but human bodies. Anyway, I don't get very excited about food, which I'm sure offends Fritz.

I guess I offend Dom also. He and his wife, Elise, were used to working for proper nobles. He considered me a jumped-up peasant, which is truly what I am. I can live with that for May's sake—so long as Dom keeps it politely hidden—which he learned to do just in time.

Nobody came to our bedroom, but the knocking and opening of the front door told us that Osbourn had returned. I rolled out of bed and pulled my clothes on. Glancing back it struck me again that I was the luckiest man born.

"May," I said. "You're beautiful."

She smiled up at me, making her even lovelier. "Thank you, sir," she said. "Tell Lord Osbourn I'll be right down."

I went down the stairs with my hand touching the stone balustrade. There were no stairs in Beune when I was growing up. If my heel caught on a step, it would be no worse than embarrassing; I wasn't going to break my neck. On the other hand, I don't *like* to be embarrassed.

Osbourn got up from his chair in the waiting room. I waved him back and sat down on the couch, then said, "Tell me about this mission you were on, Osbourn. It was your first for the Commonwealth, wasn't it?"

"It was," the boy agreed. "I was sitting in court last month and a woman, Lady Verde, claimed her sister Blanche had hired toughs to drive her out of the portion of their father's estate on Gammon that he'd left to her. I volunteered to escort Verde back and take a look at the situation."

Dom came in with wine from a vintage that May had just bought on Fritz's recommendation. From the pleased expression Lord Osbourn assumed at his first sip, May had gotten very good value for the considerable expense.

I said, "Was there any doubt about the will?"

"Jon's experts didn't think so," Osbourn said. "Blanche didn't send representatives, though she can appeal if she wants to."

Osbourn shrugged. He's a trifle taller than I am and now that he's starting to fill out he's a darned impressive specimen. "The situation on Gammon was pretty much the way Lady Verde had described it. Blanche had three toughs but their shields were crappy and I didn't spend any time discussing the situation. The third one tried to throw his weapon down, but I'd already started my stroke. I stayed around a few days to see that things were sorted out, then came back to report to Jon."

May came down then. "Osbourn was just telling me about his mission," I said.

"The past may be interesting," May said, "but what I'd like to hear is whether you're going to be able to stay in Dun Add for a while, Pal? Lady Bedelia is giving a dinner party in ten days and I don't know if I should accept her invitation."

Bedelia was another of the ladies in waiting, and Lord Moncrief's companion. Moncrief was a Champion and a decent fellow, but we'd never been close.

"Love," I said, "Jon has a problem he wants me to look at on for Lord Stokes. It sounds a little like the cyst Osbourn and I got Guntram out of, which is why Jon asked me into it. Stokes has a Maker who thinks a lot of his own skills, though, and at any rate I doubt he was going to overlook any problem that way that I'd be able to solve, so it struck me that this might be the way to get Guntram back to normal. Back to what he was before the cyst trapped him."

"If you send Guntram, you won't have to go yourself, then?" May said hopefully.

Before I came up with a polite response, Lord Osbourn said, "Pal would never let Master Guntram go out by himself, Cousin May."

But then he turned to me and said, "But you know, Pal—you don't have to escort him unless you want to—*I* could. If you trust me, I mean."

"I certainly trust you on a job like this," I said. The truth was, an excuse for missing Lady Bedelia's dinner party certainly had sounded good; but that was a truth I didn't plan to state aloud.

I smiled at May and said, "It seems that we can make the party after all. I'm planning to go out on general patrol but there's no reason that can't wait another ten days."

Osbourn seemed really cheerful at the prospect. "Stokes and Master Beddoes say they'll be ready at midday tomorrow. Suit you?"

"Oh, yes, milord!" Osbourn said. "Thank you so much for this opportunity, sir."

"Then after dinner I'll go talk to Guntram," I said.

"I'm glad things have worked out so well," May said. She certainly seemed pleased, so I guess I was too. Despite the dinner party.

The image on Guntram's door sounded happy to see me. Ancient machines certainly can have personalities, but I'm not sure that all of them do. The various doorkeepers that Guntram repaired to keep people away from his quarters had always seemed to me to be joke rather than serious working machines—the way a boat is, for example. But I hadn't made a real study.

Guntram was really glad to usher me in. "I wasn't expecting you tonight, Pal," he said. Then frowning added, "I hope all is well with you and May."

"Everything's fine," I said. When things were going badly at home I sometimes spent the night in Guntram's workroom. The atmosphere was pretty similar to my surroundings on Beune after Mom died, leaving me alone in the house and a barn furnished with the Ancient artifacts I'd found in the Waste—and repaired if I could.

"Thing is, Guntram, I volunteered you for a job I didn't think I could handle and figured I ought to tell you," I said. "You go off with Lord Osbourn as escort to Midian, to free a bride who was kidnapped on her wedding day and is being held behind a clear barrier for the past twenty-five years. The fiancé has a Maker who says a Maker can't penetrate the barrier—which means he can't. Like I said, I volunteered you. The fiancé, Lord Stokes, is important to Jon. I figure if I had to be close to Stokes and his Maker any length of time, I'd say or do really the wrong thing."

"I appreciate your confidence, Pal," Guntram said, "but I'm afraid it's misplaced.

"Since I came back from that cyst, I haven't been the same man."

I looked for a moment at a clock which kept time by three different systems, none of them familiar, depending on whether the digits show blue, yellow or green. I have always been amazed that Guntram had gotten it running again by replacing missing atoms according to the ghostly pattern in his mind that showed him what those atoms should be.

"Guntram," I said. "You haven't come back. Not really. I'm hoping that a tricky problem with a smart aleck watching you will bring you closer to the man who rebuilt this clock."

I gestured.

Guntram smiled, which I took for a good sign. He said, "The clock is completely useless, you realize."

"I realize we don't know how to calibrate it yet," I said. "As a piece of craftsmanship, I don't know its equal, though.

"And Guntram?" I went on saying more than I'd intended to. "The Leader believes in big things—Mankind and the Commonwealth, that sort of thing. Maybe I did too, when I was a kid. Now you and I believe in the work. The work is real."

I pointed to the clock again. "This is real," I said, "and I want to see more work like it."

Guntram sighed. "I'll be at landingplace at noon," he said. "And I'll try not to embarrass Dun Add before these provincials."

"Thank you, friend," I said and headed back for home.

I didn't know whether or not Guntram would succeed on Midian, but I'd succeeded in getting Guntram moving. That had been my job, and it was much more important to me than anything concerning Lord Stokes.

Several days later, I returned to the chambers of the Chancellor. There was now a waiting room in place, but admission was controlled not by a clerk but by a Champion, Lord Manzas. I realized the increasing bureaucracy was a sign of the Commonwealth's success, but I looked back fondly to the days when seeing the Chancellor was no more complicated than dropping in on my neighbor Gervaise on Beune.

"He'll be a while, Pal," Manzas said. "Going to take long?"

"I don't think so," I said. "I'm just checking in for politeness before I ask Mistress Toledana for a patrol route."

Somebody was shouting on the other side of the far door, which surprised me. Clain wasn't a person you shouted at: not only was he Jon's Chancellor, he was a warrior of unmatched skill. I had risen to my present stature by cleverness and hard work. Clain was certainly clever and worked hard, but he's become the paramount Champion by virtue of crushing everything in his way. He is strong, quick, and instinctively does the things I had taught myself to do by studying warriors like him.

A heavy man in expensive clothes came out. I thought he was Count Osbert. Through the door before it closed behind him, I saw Clain advancing. The scene suggested that the visitor had gone out the door before Clain hurled him through it.

"Didn't take as long as I figured," Manzas said. "You want to go through now, Pal, or wait a bit?"

The visitor stomped past us, making a point of stamping his feet every time they came down. "I'll chance it now, Manzas," I said and walked to the door. Those already waiting watched me but nobody contested my primacy.

I tapped and Clain grunted, "Come!" through the door.

I opened it wide enough to meet the Chancellor's eyes and said, "Is this an all right time to see you briefly, sir?"

"Come on in, Pal," Clain said. "Unless you think I should make you regional overlord because you're so important, it's a fine time. I suppose you're here to check on Lady Irene? She's fine, but take a chair."

I did take the seat Count Osbert had shoved backward when he leaped to his feet, but I said, "I finished with Lady Irene when I delivered her to Dun Add. I'm glad she's doing well, but I came for your approval of me asking the Clerk of Here for a patrol route in a region she thinks would benefit from the Commonwealth's attention. Or perhaps you have your own choice?"

"Nothing's been squealing for attention so loudly I've heard it," Clain said. "But Mistress Toledana might've heard something before I would. Work it out between the two of you."

He rubbed his bristly chin and went on, "As for Irene, she's rented the second floor of a building in the city, above some upscale shops. She proposes to teach women to become Makers. Louis tells me that's not possible, but it seems a harmless business to me."

"I understand what Louis means," I said, "but the lady certainly does something and calling it being a Maker seems pretty accurate."

I shrugged and added, "It seems harmless to me too. Has she gone back to Master Sans's workshop for more equipment, do you know?"

"I haven't any idea," Clain said. "The only reason I know as much as I do is that the lady is renting the property from me. I wondered whether there were enough women wanting to be Makers to make the effort pay, She told me that there are wealthy widows who view this as an alternative to getting more involved in church work, and some of them sponsor younger protégés. Also there are very ordinary working women who see this as a way to better themselves. The charwoman who does for Irene is trading her services for lessons."

Clain shrugged. "In any case, I don't see it as a concern for the Commonwealth, unless Jon tells me it is."

"I wish her well," I said as I got up again. "I'm just glad she's out of my hair—and also Morseth's. I'll go chat with Mistress Toledana and find a reasonably useful way of staying away from dinner parties and the like."

I left Clain's office and headed up to the Clerk of Here on the top level of the north wing.

The Clerk of Here's office contained a great deal of floor space, but what it mostly contained were paper files of one sort or another. After the reception clerk at the entrance, I saw only half a dozen people using the ranks of cabinets as I walked briskly through the aisle I took to the back. They were probably staff working out routes for the few querents in reception.

Mistress Toledana was one of the most important people in the Commonwealth; she had a complete listing of the entire Road network in the Commonwealth and as far beyond as people had reported back to her. Unlike the Chancellor, however, her office got very little traffic. Most people didn't want to travel out of Dun Add once they had reached it. I was unusual in feeling the romance of nodes as minor as Beune itself was.

I rapped on the door in the far wall. "Come on out," the Clerk called. "The breeze blew the door shut."

Mistress Toledana's office was cantilevered off the side of the palace. The timbers supporting it were as sturdy as those support-ing the roof. Nonetheless, I was never comfortable coming out here with her. It's what she wanted, though, for whatever reason.

She was glad to see me, smiling and saying, "Pal? It's always good to see you. You were on a general patrol, weren't you? Have you reported yet?"

"I asked Baga to do that," I said. "But I just sent him off in the boat, so if he didn't I'll try to fill out the form myself. There really isn't much to say except that we got off in a region linked to Here but only accessible by a Maker doing something I don't understand. It's surrounded by the Waste, but I don't know how it connects with Here or if it does."

"Jot all that down on your way out," she said. "I'll figure out how to file it later."

"What I'm really seeing you for," I said, "is a new foot patrol route. Do you have someplace that you'd like to know more about?"

Mistress Toledana looked hard past my left shoulder. "Look, seeing it's you, Pal, and you're not very fussy...?"

"Not a bit," I agreed. "I told Jon when he made me a Champion I'd go where he sent me. My job was to go where he thought I'd be useful. Lord Clain said you'd decide that for me."

"Well, in that case," the Clerk said, "I've had my people rough out a route along the western Marches. It's mostly outside the Commonwealth at the moment. It's a hike to get there, though. You'd save yourself a lot of effort by taking your boat to Arpitan and jumping off from there. It's got a nice inn."

"The boat's carrying Guntram and the local ruler off to Midian where there's a problem," I explained. "Jon is expecting Midian to come into the Commonwealth if Guntram makes things work out."

"So it'll be just you and Baga?" Mistress Toledana said.

"I'll borrow Jon's boat," I said. "I don't have as good a memory for routes as Baga does but I'll take the itinerary your people send me with and jot down notes as I go."

She sighed and said, "You've always known what you're doing, but you're really going to be roughing it this time, Pal, once you get past Arpitan. There isn't a rush on this, so if you wanted to wait till you got the boat back, nobody'd care."

"Thank you, mistress," I said as I went back inside the building. "But the truth is, I kinda like being off on my own now and again."

CHAPTER 7

To the Southwest

Sam, Baga, and I reached Arpitan in the late afternoon. According to Mistress Toledana's note and what folks in Arpitan said the next node on was the better part of a day beyond, so I elected to spend the night here and jump off in the morning.

Which at dawn we did. The Road branching left out of Arpitan got very little traffic and had narrowed to the point that I doubted two men could've walked abreast. We were in good spirits. It was good to be beyond the Commonwealth.

We reached three minor nodes just off the Road. One was so little used that Sam noted only a vertical line in the Waste. I tugged him to take it. The node was little more than ten feet across, forested and really interesting only because one edge was washed by a stream. I filled my water bottle for me and Baga and scraped a bowl in the clay to make it easy for Sam. He emptied it twice.

Nobody in Arpitan had mentioned it and it was at least possible that they didn't know the node existed. It could be a useful source of water for a body of troops or emigrants passing through. I jotted it down on the margin of my itinerary. The second and third nodes were equally small but were actually on the Road rather than just off it, though they had no amenities—not even water. They were already on the itinerary. I thought of building a small campfire, but we had nothing to cook except the sausage, cheese and biscuit we'd brought from Dun Add. We didn't need to rest our legs yet. There was supposed to be a proper inn at Waltherius so Baga and I pressed on.

The itinerary said that Waltherius had about sixty people in two communities. There were only a dozen houses in this one, but one had a loft and a barn which I hoped was the promised inn. I headed for it.

The door gave only onto a common with a bar on the left end and a fireplace, cold at present, on the right. There was a man on a bench near the fireplace holding what looked like a face mirror. I didn't see anyone else for a moment, but a boy of ten leaped into sight behind the bar and shouted, "Hey, Pa! You got a guest!"

The man on the bench looked over at me and said, "Where are you from, sir?"

"I came from Arpitan," I said. "But I was born on Beune, if that's what you mean. My name's Pal."

A heavy man clumped down the stairs. "Looking for a room and a meal for you and your man?" he called.

"And a kennel and food for my dog," I agreed.

"Six coppers for you and your man, and two more for the dog," he said. "That's full weight coins, mind you."

I fished the tariff out of my purse and clacked the coins on top of the bar. I suspected if I'd arrived as Lord Pal on a mission for the Leader the charge would have been in silver. As Pal, a traveller from a place nobody'd ever heard of, I got charged what I should have been charged. I was carrying silver in my purse and gold in the hem of my tunic, but it would rankle to be robbed.

"My name's Gelb," called the man on the bench. "I'm a farmer on Minata. Guess I'm about the biggest man hereabouts, wouldn't you say, Abel?"

"That's surely true, Master Gelb," the innkeeper said.

I looked back to Gelb. He was the model of a prosperous farmer. But that wouldn't have impressed me greatly on Beune, and it surely didn't now that I'd lived in Dun Add.

"Say, come over and look at this, Master Pal," Gelb called.

Out of curiosity rather than a desire to get to know Master Gelb better, I walked over to the couch and looked more closely at what I'd taken for a mirror. Instead of reflecting the interior of the common room, the polished bronze face showed me the yard of a prosperous farm—like that of Squire Groves on Beune.

As soon as I took the handle of the mirror, I knew what I had. To Master Gelb I said, "This is an Ancient artifact and it's been restored by an expert Maker. Where did you get it?"

"Well, who are you to ask!" Gelb said, jerking the artifact back from me.

"Sir," I said, stepping away and raising my hands palms out. "I misspoke. I'm a Maker myself in a small way and was startled by the excellence of this workmanship. I would very much like to meet the Maker who accomplished it. He's on Minata, then?"

I recalled the name Minata from the list of nearby nodes on the itinerary the Clerk of Here had provided for me, but I would certainly need a guide if I were to go there myself. I wondered if Gelb would guide me?

"He is not," the farmer said, relaxing slightly. "He lives in a node not far from here, but I don't know that it has a name. It used to be Not-Here when Abel opened the inn, and it's still pretty much a desert, but Sime moved in right away. Do you know a name for it Abel?"

"I do not," said the innkeeper. "It's off the way to Basnight on the West road from here, the first right turning. He comes by often enough—Sime does, I mean."

"Right," said Gelb. "It's here I found him, three months back it must be, and arranged to buy this mirror. I can watch my farm from wherever I am!"

"You can indeed," I said in a positive voice, to keep him in a good mood. "If I may ask, sir? How much did you pay? The price would have been in gold, I'm sure."

"Gold isn't any good here," Gelb said scornfully. "I offered him a year's subsistence and the delivery costs. That's something that actually counts."

"I see," I said, imagining that a stranger came to Beune and offered to pay for something in gold. Not that there was anything in Beune that anyone would want that much. "Nonetheless I would very much like to meet Master Sime. Is there someone who would guide me to his node for...say, a silver Rider?"

The innkeeper blurted, "For *silver*? My lad Georges'll do that. Hell, for silver I'd just about close up and guide you myself."

"Georges will be fine so long as he knows the way," I said.

Abel walked to the front door and bellowed, "Georges! Got a job for you!"

He turned to me again and said, "Georges makes the run two or three times a week, carrying up the loads for Master Gelb. If you can wait a minute I'll make up a bag of spices for Georges to take up."

A boy just into his teens clomped up on the porch. "So what is it you got now?" he demanded.

"A bit of luck for you, boy," Able said. "The master here's going to pay you in silver to guide him to Master Sime. Can you handle that?"

In a few minutes I'd recovered Baga and Sam from the barn and we were off again, Georges carrying a leather sack and two loaves of fresh-baked bread. Gelb apparently staged his payments to Master Sime through the inn. I suspected that livestock was driven up at intervals, to be salted down after slaughtering at the far end.

"Do you have to carry a lot of salt?" I asked Georges.

He shook his head. "Mostly bread and firewood," he said. "Master Sime says he keeps meat from spoiling without salt."

"He does?" I said. Castle Ariel, which I'd taken back from the monster from the Waste who'd made it his lair, had a large chest which did that. The castle had also many other artifacts that I'd never heard of elsewhere.

"What other Ancient artifacts does Master Sime have?" I asked.

"Don't ask me," Georges said. "I keep away from that weird stuff."

That was a normal layman's attitude. Folks in Beune thought I was weird, but they'd known my mom and dad all their lives. I won't say Beune was proud of me, but folks weren't bothered to have me around.

The node we were going to was within fifteen minutes of the inn. I'd been told that it had recently been Not-Here, but the boundary with Here had recently drawn back and the node was suitable for human settlement again. It was largely barren, though, just in the beginnings of being colonized from nodes of Here which had been adjacent to it before the Ancients shattered the Cosmos into the place we now lived in.

Where we lived, and into Not-Here the Beasts lived.

On the node it was easy to follow the tracks of sheep walking in across the barren ground. A man rose to his feet a hundred yards ahead of us. He was in his forties and looked gaunt. Beside him was a machine on four legs. It had the sheen of metal or crystal.

Georges called, "Master Sime!" and waved one of the long bread loaves he was carrying. "There's a fellow here to meet you, and I brought a little wood and some bread."

A second machine like the first got up and stood at Sime's other side. "Georges!" I said. "What are those with him?"

"Oh, those're his dogs," the boy said. "I just forget they're around."

Sam had noticed the machines. He kept walking on but I heard his low-pitched growl. It came from his chest, not his throat. I wondered if I should have my weapon out.

That would probably send the wrong signal. I took my left hand out of the pocket and waved my right, calling, "Good afternoon, sir. I'm Pal of Beune and asked to meet you after Master Gelb showed me the viewer you'd made for him. I'm not an enemy."

"I know that," Sime said. His voice was rusty. "If you were, the dogs would tear your throat out. They sense what you're thinking." He stroked the neck of the machine on his right. From up close the creature's surface seemed more liquid than metallic.

"They're Ancient artifacts, then?" I said.

"I don't think so," Sime said. "I believe they were originally made in Not-Here by those we call the Beasts."

"I didn't know that human Makers could work on the creations of the Beasts," I said. "You're able to?"

I had come to know one particular Beast quite well. He had saved my life and I had repaid him. I didn't have the reaction of most humans in seeing the inhabitants of Not-Here as dangerous monsters to be killed if possible—or fled from if not. They were utterly different, however, and so far as I knew even Guntram could do nothing with the Beasts' work.

"Pretty evidently, I can," Sime said, continuing to stroke the mechanical dog's neck. "Come," he added, turning. "I'll show you the real reason I came to a node that had been Not-Here until recently."

When we walked over the rise I saw the sea lapping a shingle beach. "Is the water salt?" I asked.

"It is," Sime said. "Sometimes a log washes up, I suppose from

Not-Here. That doesn't matter, but the Waste has been bringing up artifacts here for a very long time. While this was still Not-Here, I'm sure."

There was a large tent farther down the beach. The sides were weighted down with shingle. Beside it was a chest like the one I'd seen—and now owned—at Castle Ariel; it was too big to move or I'd have brought it back to Dun Add for Guntram. The side facing us wasn't original but appeared to be silicon glass or some other crystal.

"I found the dogs covered legs-up in the shingle and dug them out myself and repaired them," Sime said. "The chest was on its side, the other side. When we first noticed it, I got six men at Waltherius who helped me carry it out of the water to where it is now. I paid them with the sort of baubles that I traded to Gelb."

I walked to the chest and put the flat of my hand against the repaired side. I put myself into a light trance to view the structure. The surface molecules were silica as I'd expected but the patterns below included several metals. More interesting were the gaps I found in the structure where there should be an atom but I couldn't find one. Yet *something* was completing the crystal.

"How do you fill out the structure?" I asked.

Sime shrugged. "Materials I find," he said. "The usual way."

"I'd really like to bring you to Dun Add," I said. "To meet some of the Makers there. You have a great deal to teach them."

"I'm not interested in leaving," he said. He turned toward the lapping salt water and said, "I have to remain in this place to bring my wife back."

"Where has your wife gone?" I asked, wondering if there was a way I could turn this new situation to my advantage in getting Sime to Dun Add. If his wife wanted the high life of the Leader's court, I could certainly introduce her to May—or even the Consort herself.

"Not far," said Sime. He threw open the chest we were standing beside. I looked within. There was a hog carcase missing the right ham, and the body of a woman of around forty. Her face was wasted looking and her cheeks had fallen in.

"Your wife is dead?" I said. Baga jumped back.

"Until I bring her back," Sime said. "She died while I was repairing the chest, but I'd gotten it working and put her in it immediately. She doesn't deteriorate in the chest, you see."

"I see that," I said. "But she's dead, isn't she? Ah—I'm very sorry."

"I'll bring her back with the artifacts I'm finding here," Sime said, sounding very confident. He closed the lid of the chest again. "And I'm not leaving until I do."

I thought hard before I spoke again. Master Sime had done work that was beyond Guntram—or any other Maker I'd ever heard of. I couldn't say that bringing his wife back to life was beyond his ability.

But the difference between alive and dead was more than a difference of quality: it was a difference of kind, the difference between stone and the Waste.

"Sir," I said. "You are a marvelous Maker. My friend Master Guntram in Dun Add is also very skilled. He might be able to teach you some things. Certainly he could learn from you."

"This Guntram?" Sime said. "Do you think he'll be able to bring my Myrrha back to life?"

I considered lying. I remembered he'd said his dog could read intent, but that wasn't the main reason I said instead, "Sir, I don't know what might be possible for two Makers of such skill as you and Guntram."

"You don't think he could bring Myrrha back," Sime said with flat accuracy. "I'm not interested in seeing him, then. There is nothing I want to teach him or anyone else. If you'll go away, now, I'll get back to work, modifying this chest to do what I need."

"I wish..." I said.

"Please go away!" he repeated. The dogs beside him began to quiver restlessly.

I felt the weight of my weapon. That wouldn't do any good. I relaxed and backed away. Sam came with me, turning repeatedly to glare back toward the pair of mechanical dogs. "Thank you for your time," I called to Sime.

Baga and I went back to the Road, where Georges was waiting for us. He was ready to lead us back to the inn but I saw no reason to do that and turned the other way. The Road branching left out of Arpitan got very little traffic.

We came to the entrance to a node. Sam wanted to enter, so we did. He ran twenty feet ahead and disappeared. Baga and I followed to find the ground fell away into a swale with a creek at the bottom where Sam was drinking.

Baga scrambled down the slope and knelt beside him. He began scooping water up in his left palm and slurping it down by the mouthful. I tried to keep my footing when I descended on the other side of Sam—upstream—by digging my heels into the slope of bare dirt.

A six-legged animal came from the opposite side of the stream. Baga shouted and scrambled up the low bank. I pulled out my shield and weapon.

The creature looked to me like an ant three or four feet long with a slick body colored dirty white. Its jaws opened sideways and were about six inches long. Baga's movement drew its attention but it didn't attack.

Sam barked from the stream bed. Baga, seeing that I was armed and the ant was only waving its antennae, picked up a fallen branch. The branch was rotten and most of the bark had sloughed off the wood beneath.

After glancing at me, Baga gathered himself and leaped to the other side of creek. He jabbed at the ant, striking a firm blow that rubbed bits of wood off the end. The ant's hard shell was smudged brown but it didn't seem to be really damaged. Baga struck again, this time bringing his club down in an overhand gesture that broke it at midpoint. The ant retreated again, this time lifting one of its middle pair of legs and rubbing it on his bulbous abdomen.

I wasn't sure he was an ant after all. The juncture between its main body, where the legs were, was as thick as the body parts.

I thought I *felt* a sound from the rubbing leg. There were tight little ripples spreading across the water. The ant backed further.

Instead of wading in again with his remaining foot of branch, Baga tossed his stub away and looked around for a better weapon. He found a thicker length of wood. I think it was actually the trunk of a sapling which had died across the creek in the low light and fallen over when the roots rotted away. It was too heavy for a weapon: Baga had to lift it in both arms to get it off the ground.

"Baga," I said. "Leave the ant alone. It's not doing us any harm."

Instead of obeying me, Baga lurched forward as though he were holding a battering ram rather than a club. He hit the ant's shoulder with it and shoved the creature backward.

Three more ants came out of the forest. They were larger than the first and had relatively larger jaws.

"Baga!" I shouted and started splashing over the creek. "Come back!"

I switched on my equipment and most Here lost definition as I went to a higher plane. The three large ants were all to my left. Baga and the first ant were on my right side.

The ant nearest me raised its front pair of legs off the ground and waggled them toward me while the long jaws opened and closed. I cut at the mandibles, the part of the ant nearest me. My weapon at full power slowed when it met the horny covering, then jerked through with a smell like that of burning hair. One of the paired mandibles fell to the ground. The ant charged toward me with the remaining mandible wiggling like a curved spear point.

I backed away and braced myself to thrust at where the neck met the body segment. Just as well that I'd set my feet or else the shock would have knocked me down. The point ground into the ant's chest, catching and jerking free repeatedly as it went deeper. The legs continued to wriggle in the air.

The other two ants were swinging around to the left side—my left—of the first one and would be on me in an instant. I shut my weapon off momentarily to get clear and skittered backward. I crashed into Baga, who was still carrying the fallen tree. "Get out of here, you bloody fool!" I shouted, slashing down at the second ant, picking its way around the one I'd killed or at least hoped I'd killed. I cut off one antenna.

I was furious. My instant reaction had been to chop Baga out of the way—which was crazy. But I was terrified at the thought of those long saw-edged mandibles closing on me and pinching me in half while I was scuttling backward to escape. Baga had blocked my route.

The ants paced forward rather than running—thus far, anyway. Cutting the antenna off didn't seem to affect the injured ant at all. I wondered if they could follow us out onto the Road.

I thrust toward the ant's right eye. My sword skidded over the surface, scoring it but not digging deep. The faceted material must be harder than the body armor, and that was tough enough. The effort I'd put into driving into the ant I'd killed was on the order of what I would have had to expend on Lord Clain's excellent shield.

I backed again. Baga was out of the way but he'd dropped

the tree-bole. I had to hop over it. The ant came on. I slashed at a foreleg and took it off with about as much effort as a wrist-thick branch would have taken. The ant staggered but didn't fall. It stumbled toward me again.

The uninjured ant was pressing me. I concentrated on it instead of taking off the remaining foreleg of the previous ant. I slashed left and right, backhand and forehand. I didn't sever either of the ant's forelegs but I cut deeply into the meat—the muscle—beneath the armor.

I circled to my left, careful not to slide down into the creek. I was planning to rush in and stab into the socket of a middle pair of legs to really cripple the ant. Baga was struggling with his tree trunk again.

"I'll help you!" he said, shouting to be heard even though my weapon had taken up from the normal plane of Here.

"No!" I shouted back. "Go the Road! We're getting out of here!"

I saw beyond Baga the looming shape of another ant coming through the trees. "Watch out, there's another!"

Baga dropped his pole and fell backward. Instead of rushing forward the ant remained ten feet back at the edge of the trees and from its misshapen head squirted a brown fluid at Baga. Baga screamed and fell down.

I rushed the creature. When in doubt I always charged an opponent. It wasn't necessarily good strategy, but it was one of two ways you could react in a sudden crisis. Running away was rarely the correct response for a Champion of Mankind, but my reaction wasn't based on long-term considerations.

This ant's head wasn't like those of the others. It was a long box on edge with a stubby nozzle like the watercock of a fountain. The nozzle was what squirted Baga, but though it turned toward me it didn't squirt again. Maybe it had exhausted its fluid reservoir, maybe it took time to build up the necessary pressure.

I swatted backhand at the outthrust nozzle. It was a hollow tube and I severed it close to the base. The ant actually leaped backward, back among the trees. More brown fluid dribbled from the hole in the ant's head where the nozzle had been.

The ants I'd been fighting previously stood half-crippled at the edge of the woods. They weren't coming after me. The only uninjured ant in sight was the small one which Baga had attacked, and it hadn't been aggressive during the whole time we'd seen it.

I dropped my weapon and shield into my tunic pockets. They had been at their highest settings for long enough that there was a risk they'd be hot enough to singe cloth or even set it on fire. I really ought to have my pockets lined with suede, but I didn't have time to worry about it now.

I lifted Baga under the arms and dragged him down into the stream. The stream was shallow even in the center—less than a foot deep. The current was swift, though, and the stones of the bed were smooth and six inches in diameter.

Baga's left arm and the left side of his tunic were covered with the brown fluid. It smelled bitter and my stomach was already starting to roil.

I turned him in the cold water so that it covered all of the stain. I tried not to touch the stain with my bare hands, instead trying to tug the tunic away from his body without touching the brown glop that stuck it to his skin. Then I pulled the tunic off his torso and used unstained portions of the hem to rub clean Baga's left hand and forearm. Where the fluid had touched him, the skin was already turning angry red and swelling.

The fluid didn't want to come off in the cold water. Maybe soap would have helped.

I was beginning to shiver with the cold and in reaction to what had just happened. The ants hadn't moved from where I'd left them across the creek.

I threw Baga's right arm over my shoulders and gripped his wrist to hold him there. I ground my boot toes into the clay and carefully climbed the bank with the doubled weight. I lurched the last step up onto the high grass of landingplace. I called, "Sam!" He'd already bounded back across the creek. Now he stopped barking at the ants and ran ahead of me. Before we returned to the Road, I glanced toward what we were coming from. Three more ants were visible at the edge of the woods. Two of them had squirting nozzles on their heads.

They didn't seem interested in us, though with their faceted eyes I couldn't be sure. At any rate, they weren't following.

Baga was moaning softly. I found that so long as I kept moving steadily I was all right. Baga's feet dragged, but I couldn't help that. We were heading off the way we'd been going. We already knew there was no help back the way we'd come.

I wasn't sure how long I'd be able to support Baga in a

pack-strap carry and keep moving forward. I'd keep going as long as I could.

Sam had initially run ahead but when he realized we were just crawling along he came back and rubbed closer to my right leg than I liked. Eventually he loped ten feet ahead and paused at the entrance to a node which was little more than a discoloration in the Waste. We stumbled out onto a landingplace at the edge of what seemed to me to be a prosperous farm.

We were at the back of a barn made of vertical planks. Through the gap between the side of the barn and an outbuilding which held a pair of wagons. I staggered toward the opening, shouting, "Help! Can somebody help me?"

I'm not sure anybody could hear me. Breath burned my lungs. "Help!"

I could see a house with a porch across from the outbuilding with a yard separating them. I resumed staggering forward. Baga seemed to have doubled in weight since I left the Road, but I wasn't going to quit now.

A woman came out on the porch. I don't think she'd heard me calling but she heard me croak now, "Help!" I waved my hand; the left was still clamped around Baga's wrist.

The middle-aged woman ran down off the porch toward me. Her dress was a muddy blue color and homespun like those of most women on Beune. "What's happened?" she demanded, gripping Baga from the left side and supporting some of his weight.

"He's burned," I said. "Can we get him to a bed? But be careful; the stuff on him may still be dangerous."

"Lord in heaven!" she said. "We'll get him inside. You ran into those bloody termites, then?"

As we staggered past the barn she shouted into the open end, "Robin! Get out here and help us! Move it!"

By the time we'd reached the porch a burly man in clogs and leather shorts had joined us and lifted Baga out of our arms. "Into the back bedroom!" the woman said. Then, when a younger woman came out the door and whooped in surprise, she added, "Bertie, bring butter from the wellhouse. He's burned."

"Thank you, ma'am," I said. I leaned against one of the sturdy chairs on the porch, sucking in deep gasps to get my breath. "I'll pay you for your help."

Greasing Baga's injuries was going to play hell with her

bedding. I wondered to what degree coined money would be useful on this node? Certainly I would offer it.

Which reminded me that Baga's purse held most of our copper. I'd take that shortly.

The woman had gone into the house. As I started to follow her she came back outside. "There's a healer two farms over," she said. "He's the owner's brother. You said you can pay him?"

"As much as it takes," I said. "Will you send for the healer?"

"I already sent Robin," she said. "But I'm glad you said you could pay. Wilf's searching for the plants he wants all the time. I know his brother Woad thinks he ought to be spending more time on the farm, but you know there's plenty folk as can get hay in. When somebody's got a fever, there's a lot fewer around who know what simples to brew in a tea to bring the temperature down."

"I'm glad of Wilf's presence," I said. "I'll be happy to pay."

And if it came to that, I was a decent hand with a scythe. I didn't want to be around that long, but I couldn't even guess when Baga would be able to travel.

I went in to see him. I hadn't looked at him since I picked him up in the creek.

There was a hemp tarpaulin beside the bed but it must have been brought in later for Baga lay on a feather coverlet. The fluid hadn't splashed his face but his cheeks were yellow beneath his tan. Bertie came in with a stoneware pot. I said, "Let's get him on the canvas before we use that." I ran my arm under Baga's shoulders and lifted him while the servant tugged the hemp under the body.

Though Baga was shivering strongly, his skin felt hot. I hoped the healer would get here soon. The skin which the fluid had touched had been red but now was fading to white.

The mistress—Madame Sarah, she told me—had covered the burns herself with dollops of butter. She was still doing that when Robin returned with Wilf, a man of fifty with only a white fringe of hair above his ears. He opened his leather case of paraphernalia and took out a bundle of twigs tied with twine. He tossed the herbs to Bertie and said, "Go boil this up, girl. We'll cut it with cold water and get it in him as quick as we can to bring his fever down."

I went out of the house and sat on the porch. After a moment

I took out my notebook and filled in the day's course and events for Mistress Toledana. After a few minutes Sarah and Wilf came out and joined me.

"How's Baga doing?" I asked them generally.

Wilf said, "Sallie tells me you want to get back on the Road. That'll be a week at soonest and two would be safer. How far do you need to go?"

I shrugged. "We're going back to Dun Add," I said. "I'm not in a tremendous hurry, but is there anywhere we can stay on whatever this node is? Until Baga can travel, I mean?"

"We call our node Elvira," Mistress Sarah said in a slightly taut voice. "And if you like, your friend can stay here for three coppers a day and his keep. Mind, I'll move him to the barn when Wilf says he's ready."

I calculated for a moment. "What say to two silver Riders on account now, new-minted in Dun Add? When I come back to pick up Baga, I'll settle up—and clear what I owe Master Wilf here?"

"Dun Add silver, then?" Sarah said on an upward note. She touched the face of the coin with a fingertip and found the edges newly struck. "All right, that sounds fair. You'll be back in two weeks, then?"

"The lord willing," I said. "I'd add to that, though, for a meal and straw in your barn tonight."

"Glad to have you," Mistress Sarah said. "I'm boiling a hen tonight. If that suits you, you're welcome to join me. And there'll be broth for your man when he's able to take it."

"Thank you, mistress," I said. "I'm very fortunate."

And Baga is even more so. It can't have felt like a good day for him, but if he hadn't been pestering the ant—"termite" Mistress Sarah, had called it—none of the trouble would have happened.

In the morning Sam and I would go another week up the Road and hope that Baga was ready to go when we came back.

CHAPTER 8

Back on the Road

I left Elvira in the morning with no destination in mind—just up the Road for a week and then back again. Just as I stepped onto the Road I met a packman about to turn into it. He had a terrier whose hindquarters quivered in excitement at meeting Sam. Sam was his usual imperturbable self, exchanging sniffs without undue interest.

"Are they in a buying mood?" the packman asked, easing the weight of his large leather pack by squatting so that the base of the pack rested on the Road.

"I wasn't peddling anything," I said. "I just carried an injured friend there and they're taking care of him until I get back. If you're honest and you've got good quality products then I wish you all the luck in the world. They're right nice people and I'd want them to be treated right."

"You're not afraid to speak your mind, are you?" the peddler said, raising his eyebrow.

"I'm a Champion of the Commonwealth," I said. "Not being afraid sort of goes with the job."

If a polite warning—which that was—saved Mistress Sarah some trouble, that was even better for all parties than me correcting the problem after I came back by, for I certainly would track the fellow down if he misused so nice a lady as Sarah.

"I'm honest and the jewelry I carry is solid workmanship," he said. "Anyway, they see it before they buy. Or do you need to approve them before I go on in?"

77

"Like you say, they see it before they buy," I said, sorry now for giving him a rough time. "My taste doesn't matter. Good luck to you, sir."

Sam and I strode off down the Road.

Mistress Sarah was the reason I had wanted to become a Champion; Mistress Sarah and my neighbors on Beune, the same sorts of folks. Ordinary people who just want to live their lives—and ought to be allowed to, without interference by human bullies or monsters from the Waste.

The Road branched. I took the left branch and noted it down. We came to a node with enough population to call it a hamlet and another that provided us with beer, bread and pickled meat. Neither had a name that the locals called it by. They said that Allingham, just up the Road, was a big place ruled by a duke. I figured I'd go there and look the place over thoroughly for Mistress Toledana, then head on back to Elvira to see how Baga was doing. My reconnaissance of the southwest from Dun Add was going to be shorter than I'd intended it to be, but this didn't greatly concern me.

I met an old woman in a worn gray singlet. Her arms were as thin as articulated bones. Around her right wrist was a bracelet of what seemed to be rough stones. As I came near her she looked up and said in a cracked voice, "Sir? Can you help me for the sake of your own mother?"

"What would you have, madame?" I said. Sam snorted. Now that he called himself to my attention, I realized that I didn't see the woman's guide animal. A human couldn't go far on the Road without the eyes of a guide.

"Sir, if you helped me retrieve the body of my son for burial, I would be eternally grateful," she said, bowing low.

"What happened to your son?" I demanded, suddenly alert.

"The tyrant of Allingham had him hanged," the woman said. "Duke Ronald, he's called, and never a blacker villain than he in all humanity! My son had been prospecting in the Waste at the risk of his life and found a true wonder, a mirror that speaks. He took it to Allingham, but rather than pay him the worth of this thing, Duke Ronald called him a thief and had him taken out and hanged. They left the body to hang on a little node not far from this place and would not allow him to be buried as a dead man should be, for his soul's sake. I cannot take him down myself, but with your help sir, I pray that I can."

"Lead me to his body," I said. I had strong doubts about the woman's story. I've done a considerable amount of prospecting in the Waste, and I see the items brought to Guntram at Dun Add which are surely the bulk of major items which are found in the Commonwealth. I've never seen anything really complex which has been found whole, and as described this mirror is surely one of the most complex.

On the other hand, I couldn't fault a mother for claiming that her son was innocent of the crime for which he was executed. Regardless there was no harm in helping retrieve a body. If the local potentate objected to that, he could discuss the matter with me.

She went off down the Road in the direction I'd been traveling. Fewer than twenty yards from where I'd met her was a vertical shadow on the Waste through which Sam and I followed the old woman down a track so narrow that the Waste touched my shoulders to either side.

We reached a node of only about ten feet in dimension. The surface was shingle—fist-sized pebbles as though it were on a storm-swept shore—which perhaps it was on the larger block of land of which this had been a part until the Ancients had caused a catastrophe which shattered the cosmos into Here and Not-Here—and the Road linking all.

The cross on which a man hung was in the center of the node, his face toward us. He'd been tied onto the shaft and crossbar rather than being nailed. From the grayish color of his face and the way his jowls slumped, I guessed he'd been dead about a week. The body hadn't begun to stink.

"Oh, good sir!" the woman said. "My Charles was such a *good* boy. If you will get down on all fours, I will stand on your back and undo the cords at his wrists. Please? I weigh very little."

That was surely true, and she was barefoot. I wasn't thrilled about this but I'd come this far. I got down carefully. Sam nudged my ear. I said, "Go away, boy," and pushed his broad chest back, then settled myself on hand and knees. The side pockets of my tunic swayed almost to the shingle.

The old woman stepped onto the small of my back then placed her right foot between my shoulder blades. She was as light as a cat walking on me. I felt her shift position and lean forward. I wondered how she proposed to remove the ropes.

A noose dropped over my neck. Before I could react she'd tugged it tight and I couldn't breathe.

I jumped up and tried to fling her off, but her toes had become claws and they dug in. Her grip on the garotte stabilized her. I heard her laughing.

My right hand came out with my weapon and I slashed through the cord that was throttling me. The woman shrieked and leaped off my back. The noose released from my throat. Looking at the ground I saw not only the garotte and the light stick which had served as a handle so that the woman could hold it, but also her bony left wrist and the bracelet still on it. I'd taken the hand off with the same wild swipe that freed my throat.

The woman had leaped wildly into the Waste, whose creature she—it—must be. I didn't react quickly enough to stop her and I wasn't even sure I wanted to. All I really wanted in that instant was to breathe again. My throat burned where the thin cord had cut the skin but my windpipe wasn't crushed.

I sat down on the stones. Sam nuzzled close again. I put my right arm around and rubbed him with the butt of my weapon. I was glad of the contact but I wasn't going to take my hand off the weapon even to pet my dog. He didn't care: his master was rubbing him.

I looked at the hand on the shingle beside me. There was no blood on the cut nor were there blood vessels visible in the stump. What I'd thought was an old woman was a Wraith from the Waste—not human and perhaps not even alive. Were the monsters of the Waste really machines that the Ancients had created?

I didn't touch the hand but the bracelet had dropped free when the hand fell to the ground. I'd initially thought the beads were coarse pebbles. When I examined them carefully I found that each bead was a separate Ancient artifact, though at a quick scan all I could be sure of was that they were so complex that I would need a month of careful probing to unlock their secrets.

I sighed. What I really needed was Guntram's insights. Perhaps I'd get them when I returned to Dun Add. But for now...

"Come on, Sam," I said, levering myself to my feet. "Let's see if we can find Allingham."

We returned to the Road and continued on the way we'd been going.

CHAPTER 9

Allingham

I reached a landingplace that opened onto a community of considerable size. There was no herald as there would have been at Dun Add, but there were several booths offering clothing and cheap jewelry; and one with demijohns of liquor. There was also a fellow with a peaked blue cap that looked official. He was wearing what struck me as pretty low-end equipment: a shield that wouldn't have gotten him into the Army, let alone the Hall of Champions, and a weapon that wasn't much better.

I'd have to give it more than a quick glance to be sure, but I'd seen a lot of hardware since I first came to Dun Add.

I walked up to him and said politely, "I have business for your ruler. On the Road they named him as Duke Ronald. Can you direct me to him?"

The fellow had stiffened when I approached him though I didn't wear my gear openly. My pleasant tone and smile caused him to relax a little. He gestured behind him and said, "Just go up the street there. That's Duke Street. The palace is at the head of it and I suppose you'll find the Duke there. This morning is his court day. Just go on up."

The path to the street wasn't graveled but the street itself was laid with large cobbles. The houses to either side were mostly built of brick. Allingham was apparently well forested, making wood and charcoal available to fire bricks. In Beune the better houses were timber-framed, but the walls were often filled with wattle and daub, well plastered against rain.

81

It was raining now. Not heavily, but enough to wet the pavement. In my pack was a closely woven cloak that doubled as a ground sheet when I had to sleep rough. There wasn't a good place to unpack and the rain was barely a drizzle. I decided I'd hold off until I reached the palace and put the cloak on there if I needed to go out again.

The buildings along the street were mostly two story with shops on the lower level and occasionally a business placard on an outside staircase as well. More often I suspected the owner lived over the shop.

Some people were standing in their doorways. Mostly they let me walk past briskly. An exception stepped directly into my path and offered to make me a suit out of whichever fabric I chose. What I was wearing had suffered during the trip, but it was still presentable in my opinion—and I think Baga's wife, Maggie, would have passed it also. She was a stiffer judge than I was.

"Thank you, sir," I said. "But I think these'll get me home."

I walked on, glad that the tailor didn't follow along. I wondered if Duke Ronald would take exception to the mud stains and damage my clothes had taken while I was dealing with the termites. I supposed I could buy a new outfit if Ronald was so finicky—or I could simply go back to Baga and after that to Dun Add. I thought that I ought to warn the locals if there was a dangerous Wraith haunting the Road near Allingham, but I wasn't really sure what Duke Ronald could do about it except warn people to be careful.

Maybe the Wraith had died from the injury I'd given her. That would be nice, but she had certainly seemed sprightly when she sprang into the Waste after I cut her.

Another man in a blue cap stood at the entrance of what I took as the ducal palace—the largest building I'd seen in Allingham. Wings had been built onto both sides of the original building in a different color of brick. There was a porch in front and half a dozen loungers. I started through them with Sam at my side.

"You can't take a dog in there," the guard said harshly.

I touched Sam on the flank to stop him and considered options. Allingham must have a stable, but instead I looked at the people on the porch. A fellow of fifty or so wore work boots and struck me as a farmer. The man he'd been chatting with I took for a lawyer; he was in sober urban clothes.

I said to the farmer, "Sir, I'm here to warn the Duke about safety on the Road. Could you watch Sam here for the few minutes that takes me? I'll pay you two coppers for the service."

He and the man he'd been talking to both looked at me. The lawyer said, "We can't go anywhere till the Duke gets around to calling us. I guess we can watch your dog till then. And don't worry about your money."

"Sam, stay," I told him. To the men I added, "Thank you, sirs. This shouldn't take long."

Court was being held in the large room to the left off the hallway. The blue-capped guard sitting on a stool near the inner doorway nodded to me. He doubled as a clerk and held a tablet with a list of names; the first three were checked off. There were about forty people in the room, three or four others wearing blue caps. I'd say that was heavy security, but most of them seemed to be court functionaries rather than serious guards.

The man of forty on a low dais wore black judicial robes and must be Duke Ronald. Though dressed as a judge he wore a holstered shield and weapon that appeared to be of really good quality from where I stood at the back of the room. To Ronald's left on a lower dais sat a very pretty young woman holding an ornate hand-mirror that was surely an Ancient artifact. This impressed me even more than Ronald's equipment did.

Allingham wasn't a central node but it was a wealthy one and its leader could be expected to spread himself on arms: military defense was the basic duty of a leader. Ancient artifacts didn't interest most people, though, and large complicated ones like the mirror seemed to be would be difficult and expensive to return to working order, as I knew better than most.

I was still standing next to the entry clerk. I turned to him and whispered, "Who's the blond girl?"

"That's the Duke's daughter, Lady Claire," he whispered back, "And she's got her magic mirror."

"I have a danger to Allingham to report," I said to the clerk. "When will I be able to do this?"

"Wait till the Duke's done with judging between Herman and his sister," the clerk said. "He won't like it if you bust in."

I nodded and concentrated on the trial. A man in his thirties stepped forward from a front railing and handed the Duke a rolled document. He said, "I've showed this to Bessy and Milt.

It's the deed old Waldeck gave us when he divided his land. Bessie got a copy then and hers reads just the same. Not a word about the creek."

He glared at the woman behind the other short railing to his right. The woman glared back. The slightly younger man beside her shouted, "Herman knows as well as I do that Waldeck told us both not to move the creek when he gave us the deeds in Master Quinaman's office. Quinaman would say the same thing if he hadn't died last Spring. But Herman went ahead and built a dam to divert the flow to his west pasture!"

"Waldeck didn't say that, and Quinaman's dead as sure as Milt's a liar!" Herman said, raising his voice also.

The clerk beside me and the other guards in the hall perked up, putting their hands on their weapons, but nothing worse than shouting occurred. Nobody except Duke Ronald and the officials in blue caps were openly armed.

"Daughter?" said the Duke, leaning toward Lady Claire. Claire was looking half away from the doorway where I stood. Instead of turning to face the Duke squarely, she held the mirror beside her head so that her oblique profile showed on the glass. She didn't speak but the mirror said in a young woman's voice, "So, Master Herman. Your father didn't say to you and your sister, 'Now, the two of you act like kin ought to and don't go messing with the creek after I'm gone. Do I need to put that in the deed?' And didn't you tell him, 'No, you don't. Bessie and me, we're kin without you needing to do that'?"

"That's a damned lie!" Herman said.

"You're calling my daughter a liar?" snarled Duke Ronald.

"No, your highness!" Herman said quickly. "But that mirror in her hand would be a liar if it had the balls to say what it's hinting. I swear it is."

"So you say," the mirror sneered. "You know that the stipulation isn't on paper so you can get away with it in court. Whether any of your neighbors will ever trust you again—that you *can't* be so sure of, can you?"

"I'm telling the truth!" Herman said. "Bessie, *you* know that?"

"I know that our milk has been off by a half since you changed the creek, Herman!" said the woman beside the younger man at the right-hand railing. "Our father wouldn't have wanted that and you know it!"

"But that's not what he said!" Herman continued desperately.

"Duke Ronald," the female voice said. "You're the ruler. You could put the business aside for a few days before you decide whether to make a fair judgment or one based only on the written documents."

Duke Ronald said, "Come back in two days for an answer. You're both dismissed for now. Next case."

Herman clutched the bar in front of him with both hands. "Duke Ronald!" he shouted. "She's lying!"

His own attorney was trying to quiet him and move him out of the court. "Come back in two days," the Duke said. "You're not helping yourself, citizen. Next case!"

I glanced at the clerk beside me; he nodded. I said, "Your highness, I am a traveller on the Road from Arpitan." I was from a lot farther away than that, but it might not suit the Leader to have it known that he was scouting this region. Jon hadn't expanded the Commonwealth by aggressive wars, but there was certainly concern among the rulers of neighboring nodes that his practice might change.

"I was set upon by a monster of the Waste just outside Allingham," I said. "I was able to escape, but the monster got away also and may still be lurking in the region. I came here to warn you and your citizens of the danger."

"How dangerous can this monster be if this ragged fellow got away?" the mirror said. I hadn't heard Lady Claire speak in her own right yet and I wondered whether the girl had the same unpleasant tone as her mirror.

"I took this from her," I said, bringing the bracelet out of my pocket and holding it up on my index finger. "If it helps you identify her."

"Let me see that," Duke Ronald said curtly.

I walked up to the throne and offered the bangle still hanging from my finger to the Duke. Lady Claire and her mirror were looking up at us.

"That's Ancient workmanship," the mirror said correctly. "Where would a vagabond like this have gotten it?"

"I'm not a vagabond," I said. I was definitely losing my patience with this unmannerly couple and their mirror. "And I took it from a Waste Wraith, as I told you."

I tried to close my fingers on the bracelet; Ronald snatched it away. He said, "I think I'll hold this for the time being, citizen. What does it do, anyway?"

"Hanged if I know," I said. "I just cut it off the wrist of a monster of the Waste and I haven't had time to look closely at it."

"It's a map of this region," said the mirror. "Each of the four beads is a separate map which interlock when they're expanded on the proper tool."

The reflection on the seeming mirror turned and appeared to be looking directly at Lady Claire—instead of showing the lady's profile as it would have done if it were really a mirror. "Lady," it said, "might it be part of your jewelry which you lost after being visited by an old woman?"

"It certainly could have been!" Lady Claire said in exactly the same voice—including the peevish undertone. "Papa, you mustn't let that man take my bracelet!"

"I shan't," Duke Ronald said, looking at me harshly.

I had no idea where the bracelet came from. I much doubted it had been stolen from Lady Claire, but I couldn't prove that and the claim might have been true. "Mistress," I said, looking at Claire and raising my voice. "The claim is on your soul and may the Almighty requite you justly."

"The vagabond doesn't lack spirit," the mirror said. "Lady, I shouldn't wonder if he were wearing the bracelet from your other wrist also. What do you think?"

"Search him!" Lady Claire shrilled, jumping to her feet and pointing at me. The blue-capped guards were converging on me and unholstering their shields and weapons.

I wasn't carrying another bracelet, of course—nor had been the Waste Wraith, unless it had been somehow concealed within the monster's exiguous garments. On the other hand, a search would find my weapon and shield. I'd seen enough of what passed for justice in Allingham to know that Ronald would confiscate my hardware, and without it there'd be nothing I could do.

I still had it at the moment.

I pulled out weapon and shield and switched them on. "I am not a vagabond!" I shouted. "I am a Champion of the Commonwealth and will defend myself if you attempt to disarm me!"

There were four guards in the audience and the fifth one— whom I'd spoken to—at the doorway. That last man didn't move—he didn't even put his tablet down—but other four continued pushing forward while spectators tried to scramble out of the way.

Sam rushed into the room. I hadn't called him, but he must have sensed the atmosphere. I doubted that the civilians I'd left him with had even tried to stop him; when spectators started forcing their way out of the room they'd probably moved out onto the street.

I was glad to have him.

One of the guards facing me took a clumsy swipe at Sam as he reached my side. I made a straight thrust at the guard's sternum. His shield was out of position with his stroke; my weapon cut through the edge of it without slowing, killing him instantly.

I'd been an innocent traveller until that. Now I was the fellow who'd killed a local official.

The three men facing me drew back, startled and I suppose frightened by the sudden death of their companion. The fellow hadn't been expecting a fight. His face was turned upward as he sprawled before the dais; he'd been trying to grow a beard which had been coming in a darker red than his auburn hair.

It would be bothering me more to have killed somebody so out of his depth if he hadn't attacked Sam.

That reminded me: the Duke was also armed and he was sitting behind me. I spun around. He'd gotten up and dropped the bangle. He'd switched on his weapon and shield, though I wouldn't really say he was in a posture of defense. He'd backed slightly when he got off his throne. I jumped onto the higher level of the dais so that I could reach him easily. I didn't have any time to waste or the rest of the guards would get around to doing their jobs.

The ceiling was high. I slashed overhand at his head. He blocked my weapon with his shield, which was as good as I'd feared it was. He cut at my chest. Rather than letting my shield block him, I guided his weapon away with mine and stabbed down into his left thigh before he'd even realized he was open. I hit the femur but with enough force to drive through it at a slant angle.

Duke Ronald screamed in pain as he collapsed. The guards were still gathering their courage to rush me. Before they could do that, I jumped into the middle of them, using my greater height as a boost.

Sam's vision highlighted their dithering, showing the slightest movement—even when it wasn't completed. I knocked the guard in the center backward with the sole of my boot. I stabbed high at the man on my left. He managed to deflect my thrust with his shield but it was a near thing. The elements of his shield began to fail even though my blow hadn't been well-aimed. The guards' equipment was really low-end as I'd expected.

I'd wounded the Duke seriously, probably even fatally unless I'd somehow missed the femoral artery, but it wouldn't have been safe to turn my back on him if he'd been an opponent I respected. Certainly if I had that wound I'd have managed to hurl myself off the dais onto my attacker if he'd turned his back on me.

I chopped at the guard I'd knocked to the ground, taking his left foot off at the ankle. I was trying to disable him, so that he wouldn't be in my way while I dealt with his companion.

The guard on my right thrust at me. His point skidded off my shield. His right arm was advanced so I stabbed him in the shoulder before he could withdraw. He dropped his weapon and stumbled backward.

The guard on my left, the one whose shield was now half burned out, dropped it and ran from the room. I thought I heard him sobbing, but I was sucking in loud gasps myself so I couldn't be sure.

The clerk at the door was technically a guard also, but that obviously wasn't a part of his job that he relished. He was standing indecisively where I'd first seen him. I switched off my weapon and shouted, "Drop your weapon and you'll be fine!"

He looked at the weapon he was holding and flung it away with an expression of horror; he might have really forgotten he'd pulled it out its holster. He called, "Sir, what do you want of me?"

I walked toward him so that we could speak normally. "Does the Duke have a deputy ruler?" I asked when I was within arm's length.

"Sir?" the clerk said. "Well, I suppose Lady Claire."

I turned and saw the girl slumped over her father's body. The pool of blood had run onto the lower step of the dais but it seemed to have stopped spreading. On high output my weapon tended to cauterize wounds but not enough to close a severed femoral artery.

"No, not her," I said. "Is there a chancellor or something?"

The guard seemed to have gotten the idea because he said, "There's Quinlan the treasurer upstairs. That good enough?"

"Go fetch him," I said. "He'll be fine, but don't make me go get him myself."

The fellow scampered down the hall in the direction of a flight of stairs. While he was gone, I picked up the Duke's equipment, the only really good items in the room. I had to move Lady Claire in order to unbuckle the bandolier and holsters.

She looked up at me and snarled, "You murdered my father."

"I defended myself against a thief," I said. "And you were making him a thief, girl."

That reminded me. I found the bracelet on the floor. I then stepped over to Claire's chair and picked up the mirror.

"Stealing me, now?" it said in my voice.

I glanced down at it. The face on the glass was mine with a quizzical expression. "I'm taking you back to my friend Guntram," I said. Then I said, "Did you know what was going to happen? Were you trying to get the Duke killed?"

The mirror laughed loudly and said, "Well, he wasn't much loss, was he? You got what your leader would have wanted, didn't you?"

I'd just killed several men. I'm not sure what Jon would have wanted, but it certainly wasn't something *I'd* wanted to do.

Though I didn't know what Jon would have wanted, I surely knew that he'd have done the same thing under the same circumstances. There had been no choice.

The clerk came back, leading a plump older man in very gold-embroidered clothes. "This is Lord Quinlan," the clerk said. "I told him you wouldn't hurt him."

"Royce said you wanted to see me, milord," the treasurer said. "Very little of the duchy's treasury is in specie, I'm afraid."

"I'm not here to loot Allingham," I said. "I was here by chance and defended myself when he tried to rob me. Because he's dead, I am claiming the node on behalf of the Commonwealth of Mankind, but it will take weeks or even months to get a proper governmental team here from Dun Add. I'm appointing you vicar until then. Royce, how many guards are there in Allingham, you guys with blue caps? Besides the ones here today."

"I guess ten all told," the clerk said doubtfully. "I saw Hastane run out after you killed the Duke so I guess he's okay."

"You *killed* the Duke?" Quinlan said. He hadn't gotten any

farther than the doorway to the hall, so he probably couldn't really have seen the dais and what was there.

"He came at me with a weapon," I said. "Look, Lord Quinlan, you may need more people than that. Can you recruit them? And Royce? Is there going to be a problem with you guards taking orders from Quinlan?"

"No sir," the clerk said forcefully. "Not after I get 'em in here to clean up the mess."

"Right," I said. "Tell them if I come back I'll take care of any problems. You're in charge of the guards." I turned to Quinlan and said, "That all right with you, sir?"

"Yes," the vicar said. I figured he'd agree with any bloody thing I said.

"Right," I repeated. "Royce, point me at a place where Sam and I can get something to eat. We're not going to stay long, but I figure I need to be here *that* long."

"Sir?" said Quinlan, glancing toward dais. "What of Lady Claire?"

A question I'd avoided considering. She was sitting beside her father's body, looking at her hands. "Let her be unless she tries to get involved with running things." I looked at the clerk and said, "Royce?"

"Right, sir," he said. "Then I'll show you the Ace of Spades. Then I better get back here with some help."

CHAPTER 10

Going Home

We left Allingham as quickly as I could. I was eating slabs of ham and cheese between halves of a crusty roll. Sam had eaten but he was carrying along the hambone, which I knew from experience he would demolish overnight. He had jaws that didn't quit and he was still a young dog with perfect teeth.

Allingham seemed a perfectly nice place now that the Duke was gone. The whole business had given me a sour feeling, but that was what being a Champion was all about: dealing with bullies who preyed on other people. Duke Ronald hadn't been a bad example of the type, but the whole breed had to be stopped. Otherwise people would grow up believing that if you had the strength to do it, you could take anything you wanted. Without the rule of law there could be no safety and no progress: if you created something, somebody else might just take it away because they wanted it.

In a way that was worse than monsters from the Waste. The monsters were destructive but random. People like the Duke and his daughter took exceptional items that other humans had created or found with difficulty, reducing the willingness of ordinary people like me to prospect the Waste or rebuild the rare wonders that they found there.

I was very tired when we reached Elvira and I think Sam was wearing down as well. I'd decided when we left Allingham that if Baga wasn't ready to go back when I arrived I was going to return to Dun Add by myself. I'd buy him a dog of some sort so that Baga would be able to follow when he felt he was ready to. Now . . . I was thinking that relaxing at Mistress Sarah's farm might be a pretty good idea.

"Hello the house!" I shouted as we walked through landing-place. I hadn't been aware of much when I arrived the first time, breath burning in my lungs and my legs wobbly from the effort of carrying Baga from where we'd met the termites. "Mistress Sarah, I'm back a bit sooner than I'd expected."

Robin came out of the barn an instant before Sarah appeared on the porch of the house. "Pal?" she said. "Wilf is just checking over Baga and he's doing quite well."

I cranked the hand pump in the yard, bringing up a gourd-ful for the pottery dish on the ground which Sam had shared with the chickens, then an additional gourd for myself. I walked into the house behind Sarah and reached Baga's room just as the healer was preparing to leave.

"How soon will you be able to start for Dun Add, Baga?" I asked.

"Right now if he says so," Baga said, nodding to Wilf.

They were both standing beside the bed. I nodded to Wilf and said, "Healer?" on a rising note.

Wilf said, "He should keep the burns out of the sun and covered in grease. But there was no serious damage to the muscles, so if he's willing and you're reasonably careful on the way I see no reason not to."

"Mistress Sarah," I said. "If you can put us up one more night, we'll be out of your hair tomorrow morning."

Baga started out limping. He said the skin on his left arm and chest caught him every time he moved. Sam and I had made a pretty fast trip back from Allingham, though, and weren't inclined to push. I suggested we go off with Master Sime so that Baga had the use of his healing cabinet. That would have meant sharing it with Sime's late wife. Baga preferred pain to doing that, and though I didn't agree with his decision I could understand it.

He loosened up as we walked toward Dun Add. Before we reached Arpitan and the boat he was back to normal.

We picked up a grouping which grew to over thirty people going to the city. Normally I'd have gotten past and gone down ahead but this time I was just as glad to be in company and the slow pace suited Baga.

I push myself hard and that spills over in the way I treat other people, I know. I'm trying to train myself to be more careful, though. I wasn't in a real hurry to get back to Dun Add, though I had business for the Leader and the Clerk of Here.

The first thing I noticed when we arrived at landingplace on Dun Add was that my boat was back from carrying Guntram and Lord Osbourn off to solve Lord Stokes's problem. Maggie, Baga's wife, was sitting on the little porch they'd built against it for the times it was in Dun Add but being lived in.

Baga and Maggie had a room in the city which Maggie used when Baga was off with the boat; at most times, however, the couple lived in the boat while it was on the ground. Boats aren't laid out as well for stationary use as ordinary houses, but they do well enough for a couple who didn't entertain.

I took my place in the line of new arrivals, but the Herald's clerk noticed me and Baga, then called his superior's attention to me and Sam. The plumply self-important Herald bustled up to me. "Lord Pal!" he said. "I thought your boat had arrived days ago! Sorry you had to wait this way."

"It's no problem," I said. In his absence his clerk was processing arrivals in normal order, probably more efficiently than would have happened with the Herald's officiousness intruding. Baga was getting out of the boat. "If it's all right with you, though, I'll take care of the formalities while Baga goes to his wife—whom I see sitting right over there with any boat. Baga, I'll stable Sam while you say hi to Maggie."

I rubbed Sam behind the ears and made minimal responses to the Herald's questions as he filled out the arrival questionnaire. Baga didn't so much scamper as shamble over to the boat where Maggie greeted him as soon as she heard him calling her. They were both waiting for me as soon as I'd processed through arrivals. "Come over and have a mug of your own fine lager with us!" Maggie said. "May'll still be up with the Consort at this hour of the afternoon."

I really did want to take care of my business at the palace but it would be a while before May was free of her duties to Jolene. "Sure," I said, truthfully but with a bit more enthusiasm than I felt. "I'll have a mug."

The boat's converter turned any organic materials into food and drink—of excellent quality now that Guntram and I had brought the vessel up to original specifications. The texture of the food was still that of wet sawdust, but if you kept your eyes shut, the taste and smell told you that you were eating fine entrees. The lager that ran from the taps was every bit as good as that I'd grown up drinking on Beune.

The mugs were earthenware rather than the boat's own extrusions. That was Maggie's whim. It made her feel homelike and it didn't matter to me. I don't know what Baga thought about it or if he did.

"I need to see how Guntram and Lord Osbourn made out on Midian," I said as I sipped the lager, feeling myself relax. I liked being on the Road but when I was on duty (and that was always since I'd become a Champion) there was always a touch of stress to the situation. When I returned to Dun Add, that pressure came off.

"Well, they didn't," Maggie said. "Didn't succeed in whatever it was they went to do, I mean. They're both back all right, though. Lord Osbourn came over looking for you, Pal, when he didn't find you at home or in the palace."

I tossed off the remainder of my beer. "Time for me to be moving, then," I said. "I'll be going back to the townhouse after I've taken care of my business at the palace. Thank you for the lager, Maggie—and remember Baga got burned."

We'd left Sam outside with a bowl of water. He wagged his tail when I clucked my tongue to him and bounded to me as I started through the belt of buckeyes separating landingplace from the end of South Street and the city of Dun Add proper.

I thought about walking this direction with Buck when I first arrived in Dun Add, so completely out of my depth that I didn't know it. I'd imagined that the Leader's court was just a larger version of Beune. I'd thought the shield and weapon I'd made myself from Ancient artifacts that were intended as an umbrella and a rock drill were in a league with the purpose-built equipment of the Hall of Champions—not as good probably, but in a league. The Leader's palace on the high ground around which the city had grown up was the most wondrous building human beings could create and the Champions of Mankind were supernormal beings with no human flaws.

I was a Champion now and I certainly had flaws. I had equipment as good as any in Here but that wouldn't have fitted me for the Hall had I not practiced long and hard against other Aspirants and also with the machines which mimicked human opponents at varying levels of skill.

The world that I'd entered two years ago no longer existed. It had never been real except in my head. It isn't so much that I'd changed as that I was no longer deluded to the same extent. I was far better off now; but having said that, I missed some of the wonder which had lain over the world I'd been born and raised in. Everything had been possible then. I knew that wasn't true now, and the fact that I could really accomplish much more than I could have two years ago didn't fully repay me for the loss of my dreams.

Sam and I entered through the tunnel under the south wing, giving access to the central courtyard. The attendant was technically a guard but he'd been retired from the army with arthritis. He could direct strangers and kept his dignity. I knew him well enough to say, "Hi, Leon," at the mouth of the tunnel. "I'm just putting Sam up myself today and then up to report."

"You're a lucky man to have Lady May," Leon wheezed. "Tell her Old Leon sends his best!"

"I'll do that," I said as I walked out into the sunlight. Everybody knew and liked May. I was indeed very lucky. But even there, having the most lovely and accomplished woman in Dun Add as my companion wasn't entirely the stuff of romance as a teenaged kid might have imagined. The reality was better than a dream...

But...

It was a sunny day, so the courtyard was busy if not crowded. Probably as many people lived in the palace as there were in the whole of Beune. There was washing hung on permanent lines, and kids playing. There were two semi-organized games of football. There were no fixed lines, but everybody seemed to be staying good-humored.

The stables were most of the north wing and I knew there was a large stockade outside the walls of the building. The practice hall had outgrown its masonry as well as Guntram and other Makers continued adding practice machines for Aspirants to work with. Practice couldn't give a warrior genius, but it allowed somebody with modest talent to stay alive on the field against better men.

Sam was familiar with the palace stables. He wasn't enthusiastic about being boarded there, but he'd be fed properly and exercised even on days I didn't get by to see him. The staff liked me and liked Sam, and they knew I tipped well. It was the best choice for him while I was in Dun Add.

"How long this time, Lord Pal?" the hostler called from behind his counter when I entered.

It was a moment before my eyes adjusted to the reduced light inside but I recognized his voice. "Call it three days, Henri," I said. "But that's a wild guess until I've talked to the Leader."

And to Guntram. And to May. And to any number of other people, but especially to May.

"The next handler on the rota is Mildred," the hostler said. "That okay or do you want somebody else?"

"Mildred's fine," I agreed. The girl was already on the way down from an upper level. She looked about twelve—and in fact could have been that young—but she loved animals and got along particularly well with Sam.

"Glad to see you again, Lord Pal," Mildred said, fixing her short lead over Sam's head. He probably didn't need it, but it'd be foolish to take chances in the stables where there are so many dogs concentrated. "Have you seen Buck recently?"

"Not since we last spoke," I admitted. Buck was in retirement in Beune since he'd been injured in action. I should spend more time with him, just as I should spend more time with May—and more time in Dun Add with Guntram and with Jon, both of whom were friends who liked my presence.

Buck was where he should be, with the man who'd bred him. But Beune was a long way from any place likely to need a Champion. Still, I needed to see him again soon.

Guntram's workroom was on the top floor of the north wing so it was closest to the stables of all the people I needed to see, but I crossed the courtyard on the way to the Consort's suite. Lady Jolene liked the view down from her roof garden. I didn't like heights especially, but nobody cared.

The attendants and guards I met in the corridors smiled and muttered "Lord Pal," if they recognized me or looked down with a "sir," if they didn't. In two years I'd risen from country bumpkin in the palace, confident and assured even in clothing worn from travel. One of the pair of guards outside the Consort's suite tapped on the panel, called, "Lord Pal is coming," when a triangular wicket opened in the panel.

"Lord Pal to see Lady May," I said to the guards, but the door opened from the inside before they could open it. May threw herself into my arms and tugged me in. As always, seeing her after a long absence was a physical blow. The reality was *so* much better than my dreams.

I had intended to ask May if Lady Jolene could spare her for the rest of the day, but when I looked in to the Consort's gathering I saw that Jon himself was present.

"Sir?" I said in surprise. Then, because it was the Consort's suite, I added and bowed, "Lady Jolene."

Jon stood up, reminding me that he's a very big man. When I was a kid in Beune, I didn't think about the fact that he and Lord Clain had freed Dun Add and this region of Here from the band of robbers who held it. That was the real start of the Commonwealth, though Jon's father had created the name and the idea. The present reality behind the name was because of Jon's drive—but because of Jon's right arm as well.

Though Lord Clain was probably the greatest warrior in Mankind, Clain couldn't have created the Commonwealth as a viable entity.

"Greetings, Lord Pal," Jon said. His smile looked weary; it had been a very long time since I'd seen Jon and he hadn't looked weary. "You've just been over the border, haven't you? Got any-thing I'll need to take a look at?"

"Sir, I *will* have," I said. "There's a node called Allingham which just joined the Commonwealth and needs a new duke—or anyway ruler—and a transition team soonest. The treasurer's in charge at the moment and he may be capable, but I didn't stick around to check things out."

Jon frowned and said, "Then let's you and me see Lord Clain right now." He bent and kissed Lady Jolene on the cheek. He and the Consort really did love one another, though her love for Lord Clain made everybody's life very difficult. It was a livable situation so long as nobody mentioned it.

When an aggrieved Champion accused Jolene of the affair, I was forced to defend her in a trial by combat. It was the hardest thing I'd ever had to do, and only in part because Lord Baran was a great warrior whom I defeated because I was smarter than

Baran and because I was very lucky. On Beune affairs like that of Clain and Jolene occurred, but people didn't wink at them the way sophisticates on Dun Add might do. My stepmother would have been scandalized to learn that I'd been defending a woman whose morals were as loose as those of her sister.

Who had been my birth mother.

But Lady May had begged me to do it, Clain was visiting his own holdings and nobody was quite sure where he was. Nobody else had been willing to be Jolene's champion. I didn't approve of Jolene's behavior, but I wasn't going to sit on my hands and let Baran boil her in oil as he planned to do.

I squeezed May firmly and looked down at her. "Love...?" I said doubtfully.

She hopped up on tiptoe and kissed me. "Of course," she said. "I'll see you tonight for dinner. Lord Osbourn will be with us if you don't mind."

I followed Jon out of the suite, bowing to the ladies and courtiers still inside with Jolene. Jon turned toward me as we started up the stairs to the next level where the Chancellor's office was. "I didn't mean to snatch you away from May," he said. "I'm not as young as I used to be."

"We'll take care of Allingham and I won't have that on my mind," I said.

The Chancellor's office was guarded by a Champion named Sorly, who'd moved his desk in front of the doorway so that nobody could bull straight through. When he saw the leader himself coming up the stairs toward him, he leaped to his feet and skidded the desk to the side himself.

"My lord," he called in a loud voice. "The Chancellor is here with Lord Reaves! Would you like me to announce your presence?"

As Sorly probably hoped, the door flew open immediately and Clain's voice boomed from the inside, "Is that Jon there? Send him in!"

"It's Jon and Pal besides," Reaves called from the doorway, then added to us, "If you two want me to make myself scarce, I can do that. Clain and I were just chatting about Midian."

"Stick around," I said. "I want to see about that too, but we've got some other business first." I glanced at the Leader and said what I should've started with, "If that's all right with you, sir."

"Of course," said Jon and slid past Reaves into the office.

Reaves wasn't quite as tall as his friend Morseth but he was even broader in the shoulders. The two men had taken me under their wing from my first days in Dun Add because I was a friend of Lady May's. Neither of them had pretensions to being a saint, but they were two of the sturdiest warriors you could hope to meet; and so far as I was concerned, two of the best friends.

"I was just telling Clain that if you want Midian in the Commonwealth, Morseth and me can take care of that with maybe a hundred from the regular army around just to keep order afterward," Reaves said forcefully.

Jon nodded and said, "I'm sure you could, but I don't want to bring nodes into the Commonwealth by force."

"Yeah," said Morseth. "Clain said that too." He grinned broadly and added, "I know you got smarter folks in the hall than me, but I don't see what difference it makes. With Midian in, the Commonwealth is stronger, right? So why not? You've got the result you wanted."

"The process matters too," I said. "If people think the only reason to join the Commonwealth is because we're stronger than they are, some of them will decide the answer is to get stronger themselves."

"I'd take my chances," Reaves said.

That was literally true. For Reaves the application of force was usually the best response to a problem because it was the simplest. If there were repercussions, Reaves would apply more force.

He wasn't a violent man, but he was always ready to be extremely violent. For somebody who was strong and skilled and absolutely fearless, it was a pretty effective lifestyle. I didn't think it would work as well for me and I certainly didn't think the Commonwealth should be run on that basis.

Though you could make a case for the way I'd handled things on Allingham being exactly the same thing. I hadn't wanted to do that, but when Duke Ronald threatened force, I hadn't had any hesitation in countering in the same coin.

Ronald had tried to rob me by violence because he didn't think I was able to respond. I represented the Commonwealth, though. And the Commonwealth exists so that no citizen can be bullied into surrendering to violence. That's what the Champions exist to take care of; I just happened to have been on hand to take care of this one.

"I do have an idea about Midian," I said. "I'll chat with Guntram about it, but there may be a way to free Lord Stokes's fiancée after all."

Jon chuckled and said, "Remember I wanted to send you to Midian in the first place, Pal. You convinced me to send Master Guntram instead."

"Guntram is truly a great Maker," I said. "I'm at best a journeyman, so that was good advice. Only now I suspect the job doesn't call for a Maker after all. But I'll talk to Guntram."

"Clain," Jon said, "what we really came up here for is that Pal is back from leaving the Commonwealth to the southwest. He says he's added a node, but it needs an administration."

"It does indeed," I agreed. "The former duke made a practice of robbing travelers, at least he tried to rob me, and he was killed when I resisted. His daughter is still alive, but she should not replace him. Ah, and many members of the Duke's guard, call them the army, need to be replaced also."

"So Pal is the new duke?" Clain said, turning to make sure Jon didn't disagree.

"So far as I'm concerned," Jon said.

I'd been thinking about that ever since I left Allingham. It was normal for whoever added a node to the Commonwealth to become the new ruler, but it made me uncomfortable. I hadn't killed Duke Ronald to get rich and it offended me that people would certainly think I had if I replaced him as duke.

I had very simple needs and having Allingham's considerable resources wouldn't change my lifestyle. I knew May would like to cut a wider social swathe, but I'd gone as far as in that direction as I comfortably could. I was unwilling to make myself miserable just because I could afford to do so.

On the other hand, I'd let Jon pick competent administrators—and I'd watch carefully enough to be sure they weren't robbing people. I didn't know anybody who'd be a better choice for Duke than I was myself.

"How many troops is it going to take?" Clain asked me.

"There were originally ten guards," I said, "but I think I'd send out thirty troops at the start under somebody solid. I don't think it requires a Champion, but it's not going to be cut and dried right away."

"What would you think of me sending Deltchev with the

company of his choice?" Clain said. "He hasn't much experience in this field, but he's a solid man and I'd like see him broaden his background under relatively controlled conditions."

"Brilliant!" I said. Deltchev hadn't come to the Hall of Champions as a nobleman's son, or even as an adventurer who hopes to parley his skill into a position in the Commonwealth (which was basically what I'd done, though I'd greatly overestimated my skills). Deltchev had joined the Army as a common soldier and worked himself into the Hall by dogged determination. He'd be perfect to take over in Allingham. "He'd be ideal as duke. I certainly don't need the rank."

Jon looked at me and smiled. "You're a modest man, Lord Pal," he said. "I don't think Deltchev has enough experience of the right sort to handle that rank. Maybe after a year as your vicar he'll have gained it."

I nodded and said, "Sir. You're the Leader."

"Anything more?" said Jon.

"I'll run my notes over to Mistress Toledana," I said. "I didn't follow her route once I was out of the Commonwealth but I took good notes. Then I'll see Guntram."

"I'll take the notes when I see her," said Clain. "Go talk to Guntram."

Jon and I left together. I was headed over to the top corner of the north wing; I don't know what Jon had in mind. Probably going to his own suite to see what business might have cropped up while he was relaxing with the Consort and her circle. My job was frequently hard and occasionally terrifying. I flashed suddenly on the way Duke Ronald's court had suddenly exploded into violence.

Jon and Clain had harder jobs, though. I was executing their plans, but coordinating the operations of an enterprise as big as the Commonwealth had become was far harder.

That thought actually cheered me up as I strode down the hallway toward Guntram's workroom.

CHAPTER 11

Changing Direction

The snake-headed bird now on Guntram's door rotated so that first the right, then the left eye focused on me. Then the broad skull vanished back through the panel, I suppose to announce me inside. It didn't bother me the way it would have a layman, but I wished Guntram had a human doorkeeper instead.

Because I hadn't heard the bird's raspy voice through the thick door I rapped on the panel and called, "Guntram? It's Pal."

The door rotated open immediately so Guntram must have been reaching for the latch already. He looked good, so whatever else the trip to Midian had accomplished, it had gone some way to getting himself out of himself as I'd hoped.

"Glad to see you, friend," I said. "I came to hear about your trip to Midian, and I found a little toy that's yours if we don't decide it'd be better off that we destroy it."

I took the mirror out of my belt purse for the first time since I'd put it there on Allingham. In my voice but thinner than I'm used to hearing it the mirror said, "Destroy me? Are you mad? Do you know what I'm worth?"

There wasn't much light at the entrance of Guntram's workroom, but when I tilted the mirror slightly to be able to see the mirror's face I was clearly looking out with an angry expression.

Guntram said, "Sir, if that's the correct term. Pal doesn't care how much money you're worth, nor do I. We're Makers, however, and I'm sure we would both very much regret reducing an Ancient artifact into elemental bronze."

He looked at me and I nodded. "He has a nasty tongue on him," I said, "and he seems to enjoy stirring up trouble. I think he deliberately lied to goad the Duke into attacking me."

"I've never lied!" the mirror said. "Duke Ronald was a greedy, dishonest man who chose to find in my words an excuse to rob you!"

"That's probably true but completely off the point," I said. "You were trying to get Ronald killed and your words did just that."

"He was no loss," the mirror said. "Neither of you would be either: an old man who couldn't make the weapons the Commonwealth needs even when he was younger and a peasant who gives himself the airs of a noble!"

Guntram took the mirror from my hands and laid it face-down on the little table beside the door. The table was probably meant for visiting cards, but goodness only knew what Guntram wanted it for.

"There's no reason to tempt ourselves," Guntram said. "We really *don't* want to destroy it."

"It could be useful," I said, "but I don't trust it even if it doesn't lie. It misleads by what it says, and that may be worse than lying."

"It obviously has interesting capabilities," said Guntram. "I want to get into it to see if I can get a sense as to whether it's complete. It seems unlikely that the Ancients deliberately created an artifact to behave the way this one does."

"Was what you found on Midian Ancient work?" I said, at last getting around to the real purpose of my visit.

Guntram laughed and led us over to places we could sit down. He offered me the end of an actual couch, mostly covered with books and artifacts. Instead I took the pair of cabinet drawers off a pillow on the couch and set it on the floor before sitting on it. Guntram actually had a chair which he must have gotten out of when I came to his door because there wasn't anything piled on it.

"As for the enclosure being Ancient workmanship, I can only say that it's not like any Ancient artifact I've seen," Guntram said. "I literally could not touch it in a trance. It was perfectly visible when viewed from Here: a gray impermeable ringwall about three hundred feet in diameter with a clear panel about ten feet long in a section of it. We could see Marlene through it but she couldn't speak to us. I don't know whether she could see us or not."

"But in a trance?" I pressed.

"Nothing," Guntram said. "Neither the clear portion nor the gray. There were metal servants inside who fed Marlene and Master Hector when he was present. Sometimes Hector vanished through a rectangular frame in the back of the visible area of the enclosure. Men who'd been watching the site longer said occasionally they could see other buildings in the background of the frame."

"The final upshot is that I told Lord Stokes that I'd failed, and we came back to Dun Add. Lord Stokes's Maker was quite pleased at my failure."

Guntram rubbed his left wrist with the tips of his right fingers. "Master Beddoes is very skilled," he said, "but I don't warm to him."

"That's all very odd," I said. "Not about Beddoes, a thoroughly unpleasant fellow he seemed to me. Though I'll honor him for his skill."

"There's another thing," Guntram said. "Marlene was stolen twenty-five years ago."

"That's what Stokes said," I agreed.

"The woman in the enclosure can't be more than eighteen years old," Guntram said. "The age she was when Lord Stokes married her."

"Umm," I said. There was no comment I could usefully make, certainly not at this distance. "On another subject, I brought a Lady Irene to Dun Add and I suggested that she might introduce herself to you while I was gone. Did she?"

"No one did," Guntram said. "What would the purpose be?"

"Irene is a Maker of sorts," I said. "I'm going to see if she can help Lord Stokes's problem, but I'd be interested in your opinion."

Guntram shrugged. "I didn't help very much on Midian," he said, "but I'm happy to visit Lady Irene with you. I've never met a female Maker."

I stuck my head out the window to see where the sun was. I'd planned to be heading home by now, but May knew I had several people to see before I left the palace. For that matter, I could bring Guntram home for dinner. I was sure Fritz, our chef, could find something for an extra guest who didn't eat much anyway.

"Sure," I said. "Let's go now."

✧　　　✧　　　✧

Guntram wasn't as frail as I'd feared. I suppose I was still remembering the condition he'd been in after he escaped a cyst in which he'd been imprisoned for months. He was old, of course, but the trip to Midian had returned him into a proper mental state and that had made a noticeable difference in his physical state as well. I'd thought of hiring a sedan chair to get him the short distance to Lady Irene's lodgings, but Guntram didn't need any help at all.

Irene was on the second floor of the building she rented from Lord Clain. "Want a hand?" I offered politely.

Guntram smiled and said, "The stairs of the palace have kept my legs in quite good condition."

I won't claim that he skipped up the masonry stairs, but frankly neither did I. The door at the stairhead was ajar but instead of going in I rapped on it and called, "Lady Irene? This is Pal of Beune with a friend."

When I heard footsteps approaching I pushed the door gently open and said, "Milady, this is my friend Guntram, a Maker of great skill who hoped to meet you."

She, wearing a simple tunic, had entered the anteroom from the larger room beyond. She gave me a sour, disgusted look and said, "You brought him here to test me, I suppose. Well, what do you plan to do?"

"Milady," I said. "There's no testing involved. I *saw* what you did. I brought my friend so that he could see it also."

I wasn't really surprised by Irene's reaction; it was in keeping with the negative attitude she'd displayed since I first met her. I couldn't blame her: nothing I knew of Master Sans or Irene's father suggested to me people with positive attitudes. I regretted that, however: a cheerful outlook on the world had always struck me as a more profitable attitude even when the hope turned out to be misplaced.

"The enclosure wall in Midian I was viewing didn't exist when I went into a trance," Guntram said. "Pal's description of the way you access the Underworld reminds me of this."

She hopped to a basket in a far corner and took her sheaf of yarrow stalks from it. She saw us approaching and said, "I don't need these but they make it easier."

She tossed the stalks down on the floor, but the air above where they lay shattered jaggedly in the fashion I'd seen before.

I took my shield and weapon out—I didn't know what might have moved into the Underworld since Irene and I had left it.

The workroom looked just as it had when I left it. So far as I could tell, no predators had moved into the forest to replace the giant shrew I'd killed there. I turned and called back the direction I'd entered from. I couldn't see Irene or Guntram but I called toward the discoloration in the air, "It's all clear. You can come through."

Nothing happened for a long moment so I patted the discoloration to make sure that it didn't hide something solid now. It didn't, so I stepped back through into the second floor room in Dun Add. "I left the passage open so that you could come back," Irene said as she picked up the stalks she'd cast.

"Thank you," I said, realizing that I should have explained what I was doing before I left the others. Without Irene I couldn't have gotten back to Dun Add or out of the enclosure where Master Sans's workroom was located. I'd seen no sign of food inside.

To Guntram Irene said, "There. Do you believe me now?"

"I never doubted what Lord Pal told me," Guntram said in his usual matter-of-fact tone. "What I'd hoped was that I'd see how you accomplished it. I have no more idea now than I did previously."

"Guntram," I said. "You viewed the enclosure on Midian. Do you think Lady Irene here can enter it?"

"Pal," he said, "I can't begin to answer that, because I don't understand how the enclosure is constructed or the method of Lady Irene's talent either one. But I think it's worth a try if the lady's willing."

I turned to our hostess. "Lady Irene?" I said. "Are you willing to visit Midian where a young woman has been imprisoned for many years and help me and Lord Osbourn to free her? It would be a favor to the Leader and to me."

Irene tied her bundle of yarrow stalks together again with a blue silk ribbon. "Yes," she said. "Why is the girl being held?"

"I don't know the details," I said, "but the short version is that a Maker wanted to marry her. When she decided to marry another man, the Maker stole her away and imprisoned her."

"Yes," Irene said. "I am certainly willing to help free her."

"Tomorrow at noon, then," I said. "We'll meet at my boat on landingplace. And Guntram, let's go back to my house for dinner."

✧   ✧   ✧

Dom was standing at the front door. He ducked inside when we appeared, but instead of May coming out to greet us, Lord Osbourn did. "I was about to come looking for you," he called. "Very glad to see you, Pal."

"Things took longer than they might have," I said.

The front door opened again and May came out. I kissed her and said, "I've brought Master Guntram for dinner. Is that a problem?"

"Not at all," she said and ushered us into the house. "Fritz is roasting a large ham. I'll tell him to prepare extra profiteroles for dessert. He says the strawberries are very good this spring."

May guided us straight up to the third floor banqueting room. We didn't entertain very often, which I know she regretted. I didn't exactly dislike other people, but I usually preferred to be alone. May was gregarious, and she was extremely proud of being the companion of a well-regarded Champion and a friend of the Leader. I didn't give her much opportunity to display her status.

We weren't well suited to one another—except that we loved each other. I'd become wealthy and she could buy pretty much what she wanted—except my time. On which subject, I said as we mounted the stairs, "Guntram and I will be going out to Midian tomorrow to try to free a woman from captivity. We'll be taking Lady Irene."

"You're taking me as well, I hope," Lord Osbourn said from behind. "I'd like to see it done right."

"As indeed will I," said Guntram. "The failure wasn't yours, Lord Osbourn."

We reached the dining room. Elise was at the door and Dom inside carving the ham. May has told me repeatedly that we need more servants for this sort of situation. We have formal dinners very rarely, but that's still more often than I would like. Our compromise is that May has freedom to hire extra staff whenever we're having a real party. When we're having a few friends in like tonight, our three permanent servants are plenty. I could afford more people, but it offended my sense of rightness.

Dom brought around a tureen of fish soup from which Elise filled the bowl at each place. Fritz was a wonderful cook. I could have lived very happily without Dom and Elise, but Fritz's cooking was well worth not only his expense but the hassle of a servant.

"I'd be happy to have your company," I said to Lord Osbourn, "but I don't believe Master Hector will require two Champions to defeat, do you?"

"Nothing like that," Osbourn said. "Besides, Count Stokes's men killed him before we left Midian."

"They did?" Guntram said, putting down his spoon untasted. "I didn't know that."

"Yeah," said Lord Osbourn, tilting up his bowl for the last of his soup. "When you pointed out the city you could see in the mirror in the enclosure, Stokes put men to watching it. One of them recognized the place as on the next node over from Midian so he sent a squad there to catch him. I guess they were hoping to get into the enclosure that way. They didn't and they killed Hector besides, so they couldn't ask him."

"Idiots," Guntram muttered. "I could've told them that the back entrance wouldn't have been obvious to a layman."

"That's probably what they thought also," I said. "Which is why they didn't tell you after they'd failed."

People usually didn't like to be told they were idiots, Especially when they thought the same themselves.

"It doesn't make *your* job harder, though, does it, darling?" May said.

"No, no," I agreed. "I'm counting on Lady Irene, which may be foolish, but all the better ideas have been tried. If she fails, Jon loses a chance to put one over Count Stokes. He wants that and I want to give it to him. But I'm not going to lose any sleep over it."

I let Elise give me brassicas from Dom's platter. Quite a lot of what I've become accustomed to eating was unknown to me on Beune. That's probably good, because Mom was such a terrible cook that she regularly ruined meals. The brassicas were firm but tender, whereas memory told me that if Mom had cooked them they'd have become green mush.

Mom was a good woman and a good mother. It can't have been easy in a rural village raising a son who not only was a Maker but also had ideas above himself, but she was also on my side and backed me to the extent she was able. But she *couldn't* cook.

She'd have been very proud to see me in Jon's court, but it was her death that freed me to go to Dun Add. I sold our plot of land to our neighbor, and that gave me the support on the Road—and even enough left to support me when I hiked back to Beune after I'd failed miserably in Dun Add.

I don't spend much time with priests, but when I think of Mom—my stepmother, actually—I wished I had more belief, because Mom deserved the kind of afterlife *she* believed in.

I looked across the table to Osbourn and answered the question he'd asked on the stairs: "We'll have five adults and two dogs in the boat. She'll handle that load easily since Guntram and I rebuilt her."

"There's not another boat in all Here that could!" Osbourn said proudly.

"Well, there's one more," Guntram said, "the one Pal and I rebuilt on Beune. Lord Pal owns that one also."

May reached over and rubbed my shoulder firmly. She said, "My Pal is remarkably talented."

That sort of comment in front of my friends really embarrassed me, but it was better than overhearing Mom's friends telling her that it was too bad her son wasn't trying to make something of himself.

Some of those friends were alive. I doubted they remembered now what they'd been saying when I was ten, but they'd been right in a way: I'd been determined to become a Champion of Mankind. If I'd been foolish enough to tell anyone my plans, they'd have thought me as crazy as if I'd said I was going to learn to fly by flapping my arms.

I'd have thought the same myself if I'd known what I later learned. The loud-mouthed bully who'd beaten me to a pulp on my first visit to Dun Add had been a particularly persuasive teacher.

Dom and Elise brought the ham around. It was a simple meal—far too simple for Fritz's wishes, but perfectly prepared and the sort of meal I wanted but which I'd never have tasted if I'd remained in Beune.

I'd have been happy with the life of a Maker in Beune, at least if I'd somehow gotten Guntram as a teacher. I wouldn't have been as good as Guntram was, but nobody I'd met *was* that good except in narrow specialties. Guntram was a generalist, interested in everything—whether or not it was practical. I had the same kind of mind. I had to go to Dun Add to become a Champion, but I didn't know what that meant either until I came here. It meant discomfort and danger, which I'd expected even when I was a kid (though expecting and *feeling* danger were very different things).

Also I'd had no notion then of how it felt to kill another man. I'd done that often enough now to realize that I hated the experience.

But that too was sometimes a Champion's job.

"How do you propose to go about the process, Pal?" Guntram asked. He was enjoying the meal as much as I'd hoped he would. Food at the palace refectory was pretty good, but Fritz's meals were a stage beyond simply keeping body and soul together.

"We go to landingplace on Midian," I said. "I gather the compound holding Marlene is quite close by."

Osbourn and Guntram were nodding solemnly.

"I'm tempted to see what Lady Irene can do to the enclosure as soon as we arrive but that would be discourteous and might harm the Leader's desire to take Midian into the Commonwealth, so I'll announce myself to Lord Stokes and let Irene get on with her business. This is a very fast, simple affair the times I've seen her do it, and I'll hope for the same now.

"If Lady Irene succeeds," I went on, "I'll take Lord Stokes's request to join the Commonwealth but I'll tell him a team from Dun Add will be out to negotiate the details. He'll probably want a number of advisors with him. I could carry him back to Dun Add, but not his whole negotiating council."

"What if he reneges on the deal after he's gotten what he wants?" May asked.

"I don't expect that to happen," I said truthfully. "But if he does, there was a reason for two Champions to have gone along after all."

Lord Osbourn laughed.

Stokes had made his arrangements with the Leader himself. I'm sure Jon would send a large enough force to enforce the bargain if necessary.

I didn't hope that Stokes would try to cheat us the way Osbourn obviously did; but I didn't expect us to need help from Dun Add to keep Stokes to his bargain either.

I joined the others at landingplace a little before midday. Baga had brought Sam down from the palace stables well ahead of time. Baga had a weakness for wine, but he was neither drunk nor hung over when he greeted me. Sam was much more enthusiastic, but enthusiasm wasn't in Baga's nature.

Nor mine, to tell the truth.

Lord Osbourn had brought down his dog, Christiana, a beautiful golden retriever. She and Sam got along so well that they could have shared a compartment on the voyage if we'd been short of space. My boat had eight separate compartments so there was plenty of room for five grown humans and two dogs, but good feeling among the dogs was almost as important as it would be among the human members of the party.

Speaking of which, Lady Irene had arrived with one servant—a girl of about fourteen who'd brought a bundle of extra clothing. Irene carried only her bundle of yarrow stalks, now in a wrapper embroidered with a circle of young women flinging a straw doll into the air from a blanket.

I thought that perhaps Irene intended to bring the girl along. It would have been all right, but instead she sent the servant back into Dun Add.

The controlling limitation in how much a boat could carry was not space or weight but rather life force—though no human I'd talked to really understood how the boats calculated that. The Ancients were no longer around to ask.

Most boats had degraded over thousands of years and could no longer carry the complement they'd been designed for. My boat had compartments for eight people, but before I'd rebuilt it and replaced all the missing trace elements three adult humans and a dog had been its maximum capacity. It took a Maker to bring a boat back to specification. Most boatmen didn't even know how to call up the repair menu that was part of each boat's fabric. I'd had Guntram leading and guiding me the first time I'd worked on a boat. Without that I'd have been as much at a loss as Baga was. He was a skilled boatman, but if the vessel was having a problem he could only guess at a solution.

"She's ready to go," Baga announced from the open port. "Whenever you want!"

I gestured the passengers aboard, figuring to board last myself. At the port Lady Irene turned back to me and demanded, "Which are my quarters?"

"Milady, there are eight identical compartments," I said. "You are welcome to whichever one you choose. There are no real common areas so Guntram and I will take cells across the aisle from one another so that we can sit on our couches and discuss what we're working on, but no one will interfere with you."

"I'm glad to hear that," Irene said. "I won't interfere with any of you either."

Apparently she was just demonstrating her independence and ill-temper, both of which I would have taken for granted. I sighed but reminded myself that Lady Irene was doing me and the Commonwealth a favor.

Guntram was carrying a small case onto the boat. I offered him my arm to cling to as he mounted the steps but he smiled and said, "I think I'm all right, Pal. I'm just bringing a time keeper of sorts and a scattering of elements that we might find useful in reconstructing it."

I smiled. That was the sort of thing I hoped Guntram would bring. Working with another Maker was wholly different from working by yourself. Guntram and I meshed very well together. There was no rivalry: we were both consumed by the task itself. It was particularly a matter of uncovering the elemental bones of what the artifact had been originally. A Maker in a trance is tracing out the pattern of what a damaged artifact had been. I guess a few exceptional Makers can even intuit what the original *could* have been to make it better for its intended purpose: I'm pretty sure Master Louis could do that with weapons.

For understanding what an object had been before millennia of wear, there were few more skilled than Guntram. Every time I worked with him I gained by learning how to see deeper into vanished reality than I had been able before.

Lady Irene had chosen the endmost compartment on the port side, opposite the dogs.

Osbourn was in the front starboard cell, opposite the one where Baga would sleep when he wasn't guiding the boat. I suspected he'd want to make Midian in a single reach, though it was long enough that it would be reasonable to break it into two days.

I gestured Guntram into the compartment next to Baga's and took the one across from him. That left a pair of empty compartments between Lady Irene and the rest of us. I doubted that would make her happy, but it was as much as I could do.

"Boss?" said Baga, turning in his seat in the far bow. He touched a control and the hatch closed.

"Take us to Midian as soon as the boat's ready, Baga," I said.

CHAPTER 12

Midian

The boat was designed for travel, not comfort. The individual compartments weren't large enough to hold a gathering and the bow area with the boatman's seat had only enough extra space to allow passengers to enter through the hatch. Guntram and I used the aisle between us as a work space.

Using the boat instead of hiking the Road saved a great deal of effort, but it didn't make the journey itself any less boring— just shorter. When Guntram and I weren't actually at work on the artifact, Lord Osbourn sat at the edge of his compartment and chatted with us.

Lady Irene remained closed in her compartment the whole time. There was no reason she had to interact with the rest of us, but it seemed to me that a little friendliness wouldn't have been out of place. I hadn't bothered to show her where the door's mechanical slide bolt was concealed. I could easily have bypassed the compartment's electronic lock through the control console. I can't pilot a boat the way Baga or another boatman can, but all the vessel's other functions were mine to control.

The artifact Guntram had brought was a moon phase predictor, but it seemed to have been designed for a thirty-one-day month. I couldn't imagine any use for it Here—for all I knew things are different in Not-Here. That's not a question I've ever thought to ask the Beast with whom I'm on friendly terms.

It provided Guntram and me with good experience and passed

the time as usefully as sleeping or staring at the walls of our compartments. I came out of my trance having added a dusting of aluminum oxide to the crystalline Matrix. Baga must have heard me moving because he turned in his seat and said, "We'll be on the ground in a few minutes, sir. You want to rouse the others yourself, boss, or do you want me to do it?"

Guntram was stirring already. I'd have slipped back into a trance if I'd needed to. Shaking a Maker out of his trance by the leg worked, but it was likely to be a nasty shock My dog Buck had nuzzled my ear when he was a puppy. Because it was a shock—like being dumped in a cold stream—it had brought me back so suddenly that I'd reacted much more harshly than I'd have done if I'd been fully conscious. Buck had never done that again.

I left the dogs in their compartment for now; when we made land I'd let them out but for the moment they'd be excited to learn what was happening and likely to bounce around. Until we landed, nothing was happening.

That left me the problem of what to do with Lady Irene. The ill-tempered part of me thought of opening her compartment from the control panel. She wasn't wrong to worry about being cooped up in a boat with a number of men; though I might wish she realized Lord Osbourn and I were perfectly honorable.

Instead I rapped on the door with my knuckles and called, "Lady Irene! We'll make landfall shortly!"

I wasn't sure how soundproof the compartments were. If she didn't appear shortly I'd open the door after all; but without ill intention.

"Here we go, sirs," Baga called cheerfully. The boat touched down. There was no sound, but a sudden lack of vibration marked the contact to those who'd experienced it before.

"Welcome to Midian, sir," I said to Guntram as his eyes focused and his expression fell into its habitual pleasant smile.

"Welcome back, you mean," Guntram said, smiling more broadly. "It was on Midian that I trained to become a Maker with Master Perry, more years ago than I care to remember. Master Perry was a kind and good man, though he'd be the first to say that he was never more than a journeyman Maker. I built a great many weapons and shields back then for the Count's army."

"I didn't realize you were ever an armorer, sir," I said, surprised to the point of incredulity.

Guntram shrugged. "Money has never been my goal," he said. "But I needed to earn enough to live. Besides, at the time the Count was building up his army and needed weapons very badly. It was long before Jon and Clain cleaned the gang of robbers out of Dun Add. The Counts of Midian kept their node safe with a band of soldiers and then walled the city. Count Erlick ruled in my time and took a long view.

"I left Midian as soon as I was able to," Guntram continued. "I was never very good at making weapons and I was bored with the work. Master Perry let me experiment with other artifacts that came in and encouraged me to go off to any marked node where safety didn't require a large number of armed men, and the baubles I was making had a ready market."

"But Master Perry didn't go with you himself?" said Lord Osbourn, who'd been listening to us. So had Irene, who was standing in the aisle outside her compartment.

"Perry liked making weapons," Guntram said. "And frankly, he didn't have the imagination to do what I was doing. I asked after him when you and I came to Midian last month and learned he'd died many years ago."

I opened the hatch, then bowed slightly and said to Lady Irene, "Milady, will you please let the dogs out?"

She obeyed without comment. Sam shoved his way past us to the hatch and out into Midian. Christiana, far more polite, followed instantly. I gestured Osbourn out ahead of me and said, "I don't expect any problem, but I'll go next in case there is."

I could have used the ship's hardware to check the surroundings—and would have done so if I'd had any doubt about our reception. Midian differed from most nodes with human populations. Normally nothing much was visible on landingplace. Here Master Hector's enclosure, the reason we were here in the first place, was right on the edge of the Waste. Baga had brought the boat in so close that I could have hit the clear section with a rock if I'd wanted to.

Besides the enclosure, a walled city was built right down to the edge of landingplace. The central portion of the masonry wall was higher than the rest and was pierced by a gate, now open. I remembered what Guntram had said about the way Midian developed: the counts had started with a powerful military force, then supplemented that with a castle.

The usual straggle of housing and shops that normally fringed a landingplace didn't exist here, though there might be the equivalents inside the gates. The counts had made Midian safe for development and trade long before the Commonwealth had made the region in general safe.

I noted that Midian hadn't joined the Commonwealth, presumably because the counts had solved the insecurity problem to their own satisfaction without sending taxes to Dun Add. About twenty warriors wearing bright blue tunics were watching us and another ten or so were coming toward us through the city gate.

The guards already here were gathered around what at first I took for an oddly shaped standard on a ten-foot pole. When I looked more closely I saw that it was the head of a giant shrew like the pair I'd killed in the Underworld.

I glanced at Lady Irene and saw that she'd already recognized the object. Her lips squeezed even more tightly together. She held the bundle of yarrow stalks firmly in her arms.

I said, "Guntram, I'm going to talk to the guards. Want to come with me?"

"That's the Count, coming out the city toward us," Lord Osbourn said.

"I want to talk to the guards about where they got the shrew head there," I said. "I don't much care about waiting for Count Stokes, to tell the truth. I saw enough of him in Dun Add to last me a lifetime."

I approached the guards, who seemed alert but not as cautious as I would have expected. My own equipment was concealed; Osbourn wore his openly in a leather bandolier. Neither of us was a swaggerer and there were only two warriors and an old man approaching a group of twenty armed men; even so there was a potential threat.

"Good afternoon, Captain Tsetzas," Osbourn called from behind me, reminding me that while I was a stranger to the guards, my companions had been to Midian very recently. "I hadn't seen your standard before. How did you come by it?"

"Kilt it, like you'd expect, milord," Tsetzas said. "We get things trundling in from the Waste pretty often, though I don't guess it happened while you were here before. Master Beddoes says he thinks it's because of this fort—" he crooked his thumb at the enclosure "—drawing them in, so if you can get it open you'll have the thanks of all of us here."

"Yes," said the Count, who approached it with his Maker Beddoes at his heels. "That rat killed two men and a couple passing by who were here from Richter to buy a load of art glass."

"It was hell for quick," Tsetzas volunteered. "It got Michals when he tried to run it off the civilians and then Wolfram before any of us knew what was happening, but Wolfram caught it straight through the body before it killed him. Then we pretty much hacked it apart from the back."

"I suspect Wolfram would have run away if he hadn't realized the rat was too quick for him," Stokes said. "But since you've come back, Lord Osbourn, how do you propose to improve on your previous failure?"

"The failure was mine, Count Stokes," Guntram said. "And we've brought a female specialist in hopes of rectifying that failure."

"Then you're a fool as well as a failure," Master Beddoes said. He was turned away from us to look at our images in a hand mirror, which I could sense was an Ancient artifact. My first thought was that the mirror would speak the way the one I took from Lady Claire had on Allingham, but instead I saw the pockets of my tunic glowed softly red.

"Lord Pal," Beddoes said, "you are carrying Ancient artifacts."

"Yes, of course," I said. "I am a Champion. Captain Tsetzas, I'm going to bring my weapon and shield out of my pockets just to display them."

Tsetzas nodded politely and stepped away from me; I brought my weapon and shield into view and held them up so that Beddoes could get a clear view of them.

He said, "But in your purse there—" pointing to my belt wallet "—what is that?"

"Bronze and silver coins but not many," I said. "And a piece of hard cheese."

Then I remembered the key I'd found in the dead man's hand at Boyd. "Just a minute." I put my equipment away and rummaged in the wallet till I came up with the key, which I'd meant to give to Guntram but had forgotten until now. I showed it to Beddoes.

He tried to snatch it away from me. "Sir," I said. "You're discourteous. And you're making me angry."

"Beddoes, you're a very fine Maker," the Count said, "but remember your manners when you're dealing with nobles."

"This is an object which was found in the Waste and came

into my possession," I said, being needlessly precise by not saying, "I found this in the Waste. I intend to give it to Guntram here because I've not been able to identify it."

I really hadn't spent much time on it, though I doubted whether examination deeper than the quick scan I'd given it on Boyd would have taught me anything useful.

I didn't give the key to Guntram now because I was afraid Master Beddoes would try again to snatch it away and would succeed by overpowering Guntram. I could certainly get it back, but I might seriously injure—or kill—Beddoes needlessly in doing so. He was obviously high in the Count's favor, and I had a duty to the Leader not to offend him needlessly. That didn't give Beddoes complete immunity from my actions, but if I could avoid a cause of offense easily I would do so.

I dropped the key back into my wallet, which I strapped closed again.

Partly to take myself out of the situation, I looked around to see what Lady Irene was doing. She'd left the boat and had wandered over to the clear portion of the enclosure. I remembered what Tsetzas had said about the enclosure drawing monsters from the Waste. If another shrew appeared suddenly, Irene would have no more chance than those merchants from Richter had. I took my weapon out of my tunic again and started for Lady Irene.

If she'd been a different sort of person I'd have called to her. I was pretty sure that this—like most any interaction—would put Irene's back up, so I just walked quickly toward her instead.

"Lady Irene," I said when I'd gotten close enough to speak in a normal voice. "The guards warned me that this enclosure holding Lady Marlene draws creatures from the Waste like those which infested your niche in the Underworld. See the head which they've mounted on a pole?"

When I turned to gesture toward Tsetzas I realized without pleasure that Master Beddoes was following me closely.

"I'd as soon that you stuck close to me or Lord Osbourn," I said. "In case another shrew enters. You recall how nasty they were in your Underworld."

"Lady Marlene has drawn worse things than these rats," Beddoes said. "Six months ago there was a thing like an odd-shaped block of crystal that moved the way knuckle bones tumble when you toss them. The guards tried to attack it but their weapons wouldn't bite. I had a tool that shattered it to sand—an Ancient artifact that I'd rebuilt."

"How did you come to have that?" said Lord Osbourn.

"He built it," I said, "or heard about it and bought it to break into the enclosure. But it didn't work because there's nothing to feel in a trance. When Master Guntram—" he'd come up with us now "—and I were trapped in cysts there was part of the fabric that we couldn't touch."

We were standing very near the enclosure now. I dropped into a waking trance and gave it an instant's probe. There was nothing, just as I expected. Oddly enough that actually made me feel more hopeful of success. This was the same sensation as I'd experienced on barriers in the Underworld before Lady Irene opened them.

I transferred on my attention to the enclosure as my eyes saw it Here. We were standing by the clear portion. Lady Marlene, on the other side of the barrier, was dark-haired and beautiful. She looked younger that I was.

"Can she see us?" Lady Irene asked. Then she added, "She seems very young."

"She was eighteen when we were married," Count Stokes said. He sounded defensive, as well he might be. "That was twenty-five years ago, of course."

"Does the enclosure act to prevent aging?" said Guntram.

"We don't know what the bloody enclosure does!" Beddoes snapped angrily. "You're here to get her free of it. Maybe you should get down to business now."

I didn't lose my temper, but I looked steadily at Beddoes. It wasn't his business to give anyone orders. He pressed his lips hard together and turned his face away. "I've always assumed she can see us," Stokes said. "At any rate, it makes no sense that she should keep coming to the clear portion if to her it was just a gray mass as featureless as stone."

The portion of the enclosure nearest us was open to the sky, but farther back was a roofed structure with sidewalls but none in front. I could see into it. A frame the size of a bevel glass stood in the rear. Through it I could see a city square. That must have been the way Hector entered and left the enclosure.

"He was a Maker of remarkable skill," Guntram said. "I would very much like to speak with him."

"He was boasting of his power," I said. "It's always stupid to make others angry and envious. Though I don't understand Marlene's father choosing a landowner over such a powerful Maker for his daughter's husband."

"Master Hector was a commoner!" Count Stokes said. "My ancestry goes back to the Kings of Kish!"

"That was probably just what her father thought," I said. Stokes probably thought I was agreeing with him.

I know that I was illegitimate. I'm pretty sure that my mother was a noble's mistress. Folks started calling me a noble with no evidence—and I've let them go ahead and do that.

But the rank isn't something I'm proud of. I trained very hard to become a Champion of Mankind, and *that* I'm proud of.

"Lord Pal," said Beddoes. "Do you know what the key you're carrying is?"

I grimaced and said, "It was found in the Waste and cost a man's life. It's an Ancient artifact. I think that Master Guntram and I will be able to learn more with a little time and concentration. Now, do *you* know what it is, Master Beddoes?"

"I know what it may be," said Beddoes. "And I will happily offer you any reasonable price on my hunch. I've discussed this with Count Stokes and he will back my investment. What I will not do, Lord Pal, is tell someone else what I guess."

Stokes nodded.

I looked at Guntram, who was maintaining a straight face. I smiled at Beddoes, whom I *really* disliked, and said, "Master Beddoes, I set a great deal of store on knowledge but very little on money and the things most people choose to buy with it. I think Master Guntram and I will pursue knowledge in our own way. Thank you nevertheless."

"You are an arrogant young man," Beddoes said with controlled fury. He turned to Guntram. "And you, master, as I may say without libelling my betters, are an idiot if you're encouraging Lord Pal in his folly. You will *never* find the purpose of this key if you don't already know."

"That may be," Guntram said. "But I'm a fortunate man. I'm fortunate enough to know Lord Pal, the Leader's trusted confidant and a man with an Ancient artifact of unguessed power."

He turned toward Lady Irene, who had been listening attentively to Beddoes. "Lady Irene, you've now seen the lady whom you were brought here to release. Are you able to do that?"

From the way Beddoes stared at Guntram's back he would like to crush the old man into the ground. I kept watching carefully in case Beddoes tried a physical attack anyway. It would be a crazy thing to attempt, but Guntram had been frail even before his months in a cyst.

"I think so, yes," Irene said. She took her yarrow stalks out of their wrapper, then looked hard at Marlene again. "What happens to Lady Marlene when I free her?" Irene said.

"What?" said Count Stokes. "Well, she goes back to the palace with me."

"What if she doesn't want to?" Irene asked. "She's very young."

"She's my wife!" Stokes said. "And she's only five years younger than I am."

"Lord Pal," Irene said to me. "Unless you agree to give the girl at least a week to make an adult decision as to her future, I am not proceeding further."

"Who do you think you are to give orders?" Stokes said angrily.

"She's the only person who can free Lady Marlene," I said. "Which makes her the person whose opinion matters. Furthermore, I think her request is a reasonable one. And before you ask why my opinion matters, I'm the man who asked Lady Irene to come here and therefore am responsible to the Leader for her well-being."

"You're presuming on my good nature, Lord Pal," Stokes said.

I was doing nothing of the sort but I kept my mouth shut rather than irritate him further. Lady Irene had made a reasonable offer and I'd said I would back her up on it. If Stokes was halfway reasonable he'd agree and there was no problem.

"All right," he said. "Lady Marlene has a week to make up her mind as to whether or not to keep her bargain and become Countess of Midian."

Irene looked at me. "Lord Pal," she said, "you will stand in the place of a father in reviewing the lady's marriage settlement."

"I neither said nor intended anything of the sort," I said to Irene.

"You must!" she snapped. "Her father isn't here and she needs someone protecting her!"

"Her father agreed to the terms twenty-five years ago," Stokes said. "He signed the documents. And besides, he's dead these past ten years!"

"All the more reason for Lord Pal to examine the paperwork!" Lady Irene said directly to the Count.

"I'm not a law clerk," I said mildly.

"I have some training," Lord Osbourn said unexpectedly. "I could take a look at them. The major heads are all pretty standard."

"Yes, all right!" the Count said. "*Now* will you get on with it?"

"Lord Pal, Lord Osbourn?" Irene said. "You are guarantors of this agreement?"

"Yes," I said. Osbourn said, "On my honor as a Champion of Mankind!"

I believed in Osbourn's honor without any need of an oath. He'd risked his life to save mine.

"I'll go ahead, then," Lady Irene said.

She faced the clear section of the enclosure and threw down the yarrow stalks at her feet. The result didn't surprise me or I suppose Guntram because we'd seen the lady's work before. The enclosure shattered—less like a glass barrier breaking than like a sand castle when the tide rolls in. Lady Marlene squeaked a cry of startlement as clear dust flowed over her bare feet, covering them to the ankles. She tried to run but the dust gripped her like wet sand; she would have fallen if Lord Osbourn hadn't been there to grab her around the shoulders and hold her upright.

"You're all right, milady," Osbourn said. "We've got you now!"

"Let go of my wife, Lord Osbourn," the Count said, trying to push past Osbourn with no more success than you'd expect. I realized that Lord Osbourn was not only preventing Lady Marlene from falling down, he'd neatly blocked Stokes away from the lady.

"As soon as I'm sure Lady Marlene is firm on her feet," Osbourn said, "I will move out of her way. Milady, are you ready for me to release you?"

Using her firm grip on Osbourn's arm, Marlene pulled her feet free of the crystalline dust. She said, "Thank you, sir. May I ask who you are?"

Marlene now stood on the low pile of dust, but she made no attempt to get farther away from Osbourn.

"I am your husband, Countess!" Stokes shouted. "I have finally succeeded in freeing you from that commoner Hector's clutches!"

"I think the person who freed you, milady, is Lady Irene here," I said, gesturing to Irene as she bent to pick up her yarrow stalks again. I noticed that Captain Tsetzas and his men had begun moving closer. I hadn't seen Stokes signal them, but quite clearly the Count wasn't getting his will with the situation.

The business could easily go in a bad way. "Lord Osbourn," I said. "I think your cousin Lady May would expect us to be polite, don't you?"

Osbourn stiffened as I spoke. "Yes of course," he said, stepping aside from Lady Marlene, though their fingertips continued to touch. "Sorry, Lord Pal."

I didn't like the Count either, but making love to a man's wife in front of him seemed at best discourteous. Though it seemed that Lady Marlene's marriage was at best doubtful.

He bowed at the waist toward the Count. He said, "Your Lordship, I would appreciate it if you would introduce this lady to Osbourn of Madringor, a friend of Lord Pal of Beune and like him one of the Leader's Champions of Mankind."

"Countess," Stokes said. Apparently he was willing to be polite since I had been. "Lords Osbourn and Pal are both heroes from Dun Add who have been helping me retrieve you from the commoner who stole you away. I'm very grateful to them, and to their companion—"

He nodded in the direction of Lady Irene. I wasn't sure whether Stokes couldn't remember her name or whether he was just unwilling to speak it.

Irene didn't need an intercessor. She settled her bundle of stalks in her left elbow and stepped to Marlene and drew the girl to her embrace. "Lady Marlene, I'm Irene, the Lord of Banft's daughter. I'm to be your guide and companion during the next week while you determine what you want to do in the longer term."

"I don't understand this, Lady Irene," Marlene said. "Where am I to stay?"

"Anywhere you bloody please!" Stokes said angrily. "You're the Countess of Midian."

"I think," said Irene, "that while you're making up your mind, you could stay in the boat here with me and your protectors, those two Champions."

I thought Stokes might be about to give his opinion, but he didn't and I relaxed again.

"That's very kind of you, Irene," Marlene said. "Could we get my clothes from inside? Hector brought me things each time he came back. I don't know if it's in style because I see very few women from here."

She gestured, apparently indicating the gap they were standing in where the clear portion of the enclosure had been. Lady Irene squeezed Marlene's right hand and said, "Yes of course. Let's do that right now!"

The two women turned and went deeper into what had been the enclosure before Lady Irene broke it open. Stokes followed the group. About half his guards went inside with him while the remainder of the twenty or so remained grouped loosely near the opening with Captain Tsetzas.

I went back to the boat to tell Baga what was going on and to make sure there'd be no difficulty with another guest aboard. There shouldn't be.

Baga wasn't waiting in the cockpit; the door of his compartment was closed. We'd made it to Midian in a single reach, a hard run in a boat as loaded as ours had been. I didn't blame Baga for deciding that he had finished his immediate job and had a right to shut himself off and go to sleep.

The spare compartment seemed to be in fine shape. I assumed Marlene would want it but she might decide to share Irene's quarters for safety's sake. Though Lady Irene herself appeared to be giving me and Lord Osbourn the benefit of the doubt for the moment. The ladies were a long way from friends if they didn't include me and Osbourn, so it might just be recognition of necessity.

Guntram had followed me to the boat. To my surprise, Master Beddoes had come along also. I met him at the hatchway. I didn't know of any reason he shouldn't come aboard the boat, but I didn't like him and would prefer that he stay out. "Master Beddoes? Have you business with us?"

"I was hoping that you gentlemen could help me," Beddoes said. He didn't appear to be offended by my attitude. "You're both Makers and you've seen Lady Irene work in the past?"

"Yes," I said.

"Sirs," Beddoes said. "How does she do it? Is there some magic in her sticks?"

"I don't have the faintest idea of what she does," I said. "So far as I can tell, those are just dried yarrow stalks. She told me she doesn't really need them, though they make it quicker to get her mind into the correct angles. Whatever that means."

"She's seeing something that I'm not seeing," Guntram said. "Have you ever tried to explain to a non-Maker what it is that you do?"

I had—I guess pretty much every Maker has tried to explain to a layman. It's like trying to tell a blind man about the difference between Red and Blue.

"We've always known that women's brains are different from men's," Guntram said. "I took that to mean that women couldn't become Makers. Apparently the Ancients and our colleague Master Hector knew a different truth."

I thought of the teaching machine Irene had found in the Underworld and brought back to Dun Add. But Master Sans had reached the Underworld by himself, though afterward he'd trained Lady Irene from childhood to simplify the process.

There was loud shouting outside. I looked past Beddoes and saw the group of guards at the former enclosure scattering. Beddoes turned and looked also. He shouted, "It's a monster from the Waste! Let me in your boat."

I stepped aside and he shot past me, which cleared the doorway and let me out the tiny lintel of the hatchway. A giant had come from the Waste onto landingplace. It was built like a squat human but stood twelve feet tall and carried an iron pole half his own height in his right hand. Captain Tsetzas shouted and charged the giant. He paused and looked over his shoulder to see how many of his men were following him. None were. He shouted again and resumed his charge, holding his weapon out in front of him as if he were going to stab the giant with a spear.

The giant made an overhead swing of his long club as if he were trying to drive a tent peg into the ground. Tsetzas's body wasn't stiff enough to do that, but a layer of the man was between the earth and the clubhead when it buried half its length. The giant looked strong, but that understated the truth.

Sam came bounding up to me, sensing trouble. I shouted, "Osbourn, wait for me!" and linked with Sam.

The giant turned and walked through the opening of the enclosure. The women and half the guards were still inside. I wondered if the giant—and earlier the shrews—were drawn by the structure or the woman imprisoned in it. Guntram could tell me when things were sorted out.

The guards were moving, either to confront the monster or

because that was the only way out. The giant swung, horizontally this time. The club struck three men without slowing noticeably. The first guard was almost cut in two: the iron was blunt but it moved inexorably.

The surviving guards scattered back. I could see the Count in the background. He'd drawn his weapon and shield but he crowded close to the gray wall, figuring it would hinder the giant's swings.

Lord Osbourn came straight for the giant. "No!" I shouted. "Wait for me!"

He couldn't hear me when I was up a level with my weapon live. The giant backhanded his iron pole, shedding the guard's corpse that still clung to it. Osbourn threw himself flat. The club passed over him.

Osbourn got up on his toes and left hand and launched himself toward the giant's feet. His shield was still in its holster. He'd apparently decided it would be no protection against the massive rod. He launched himself the rest of the way and buried his weapon in the giant's left ankle.

Instead of swinging again, the giant changed his grip on the club and raised it to drive the butt straight down into Lord Osbourn, who tried to roll out of the way. The blow missed because the giant was toppling onto its left side.

I arrived in time to help Osbourn to his feet at a safe distance from the tip of the club, which was still swinging back and forth. I didn't need Sam's agility after all: the giant wasn't going any greater distance than it could crawl.

Osbourn and I shut down our weapons. I said, "What do we do with it now? Do you suppose archers can kill it?"

He looked back at the flailing giant. It hadn't made a sound since it appeared. "I sure don't want to get close with it again," he said. "Let's get out of the way and let Count Stokes figure out what to do with it."

We walked back toward the boat. Sam was at my side and Christiana had come to join Osbourn. She wouldn't have been any use in the fight as it developed but she didn't have the instinct to get involved in a brawl the way Sam did.

I looked at Osbourn and said, "You should have waited for me. You knew I'd be coming."

"It worked out all right," Osbourn said. "I'd seen how slow he was recovering."

"You should have *waited*," I repeated.

Lord Osbourn stopped dead and looked at me. "What would you have done, Pal?" he demanded. "If you'd been inside with the women? Would you have waited?"

I thought about the really serious fights I'd been in and my face twisted. "I never had good sense," I said. I'd always wanted to get it over with. "But you *should* have waited for me to come up from behind it."

Osbourn laughed and waved me up the boat's steps ahead of him. "All I want," he said, "is to make my teacher proud."

"Well, you've done that," I said. "But I wish your teacher showed better sense himself."

But the truth was, I didn't. I wouldn't respect myself if my instinct was to hang back in a fight. If the same habit of mind had rubbed off on Lord Osbourn, I was pleased.

Baga, looking past us out the hatchway, called, "The ladies are coming. They've got a slew of men along too."

I stopped and looked back. Guntram and Ladies Irene and Marlene had left the former enclosure. Behind them came half a dozen civilians carrying armloads of fabric. It wasn't organized by containers. "Where are you going to put all that?" Osbourn asked me in a low voice.

"We've got an extra compartment," I said. "It'll all fit if it squishes down. She won't be able to find anything till we're back on the ground—but she won't need anything till then."

Lady Irene came straight up to me. "We've brought it all," she said. "Will that be all right? Hector wasn't strikingly generous but over the years Marlene accumulated many outfits. I suppose we could have left the older ones, but they're all the girl has."

"We can carry them," I said. "Baga can help you stow them. But you know the Count will give her pretty much anything she wants."

"That one!" Irene said scornfully. "She'll wait a week as she promised, but take my word for it—she won't stay here with that old man."

"I promised too," I said. I wasn't best pleased to hear about Marlene's intention—or at least what Irene said it was, though I didn't doubt it. That wouldn't encourage Stokes to join the Commonwealth. But Stokes wasn't my liege: Jon was. And Jon knew me too well to imagine that I wouldn't keep my word to the girl I'd given it to.

"In any case we've got space," I repeated.

Marlene and Osbourn came back out of the boat; four of the servants holding armloads of clothing were still waiting to go in.

Irene called sharply, "Lord Osbourn? I need to return to the enclosure. Will you escort me, please?"

"What?" said Osbourn. "Sure."

He paused for a moment and glanced at me. I waved him on. "I suspect I can handle anything going on here," I said. They went off together. To my surprise Lady Marlene came over and joined me.

"Ma'am?" I said to the girl. It was the first time I'd taken a good look at her. She was a lovely brunette; and looked even younger than she had at a glance.

"I asked Irene to arrange that I talk to you alone," she said. "She's telling Lord Osbourn that she left one of her yarrow stalks behind."

"I don't have any secrets from my friend Osbourn," I said, feeling uncomfortable. I wished Lady May were here to deal with women on a personal basis because I was terrible at it.

"I don't care if you tell him anything you please," she said. "I saw him kill that giant. Is that the way he usually behaves?"

"I think he'd do pretty much the same any time a giant attacks," I said, "but I've only seen the once. But you want to know if he's brave. He is. That's pretty much of a given for anybody in Jon's Hall of Champions. You get knocked around a lot getting there, and to get up in the morning knowing that's going to happen takes something more than just courage, let alone skill."

"You see..." Marlene said. I thought she was blushing. "Irene didn't know anything about Lord Osbourn's background but she said you would. And that you wouldn't lie to me."

"I wouldn't lie to pretty much anybody," I said. "What do you want to know?"

"Lord Pal," she said, "is Lord Osbourn married?"

I frowned at her. I wasn't sure what she was going to ask, but it sure wasn't that. "No, ma'am," I said. "Who's been saying he is? They can take it up with me. From anything I've seen, he doesn't even have a regular girlfriend."

"Nobody said that," the girl said. "I was just wondering. And he really is noble? He's not just putting on a show of being *Lord* Osbourn?"

"Ah," I said. I finally understood what this was about. *I* was the phony, not Osbourn.

"Lord Osbourn's grandfather is the Count of Madringor," I said, "and he dotes on the boy. As a matter of fact, that was the problem when Osbourn came to Dun Add. He had money but no more sense than most sixteen-year-olds and he got in with a bad crowd. The fellow who was supposed to be looking after him wasn't doing his job."

That was me. I hadn't volunteered to mentor the kid, but I hadn't put my foot down when May told me I had to do it. If I'd refused, May would probably have dumped me—it was really important to her.

So instead, I'd done a half-assed job and told myself it wasn't my fault when he got off the Road. That he got straightened out was luck and the help of the Almighty—who I didn't really believe in—and mostly the kid's own grit and determination when he finally got set on the right way again.

I helped set him right. Better late than never.

"A bad crowd?" Marlene said.

"Drink and gambling mostly," I said, "though there were women too. I said he was off the Road. But that's in the past. If I wasn't sure of that, I wouldn't have let him come here escorting my friend Guntram the first time, before we thought to try Lady Irene to get you free."

The last of the servants were out of the boat. Marlene nodded to me and turned around.

Osbourn and Lady Irene had made it most of the way back but had stopped again. When Marlene faced toward them they came on the last of the way; she was carrying a dried yarrow stalk which looked to me exactly like the rest of the bundle.

The two women went together into the boat. Osbourn walked over to join me. "She's interested in you," I said before he had a chance to speak.

"How do you mean?" he said. "Because I'm sure interested in her. She's the loveliest girl I've ever seen in my life. And she's so nice."

"She seemed to be," I said, though of course we hadn't had enough time around her to make a real assessment. "She asked if you were married."

"Why on earth did she ask that?" Osbourn said.

"It seemed odd to me also," I said. "Given that the lady herself is married. But I assured her that you weren't and that your grandfather was a count and well off, and that you were just as brave as you'd looked when you charged that giant."

"Good grief," Osbourn muttered in a voice close to prayer. Then he said, "I don't think her marriage to Count Stokes really counts, do you?"

"My opinion scarcely matters," I said. "I'm not a priest or a lawyer. I can tell you that Count Stokes thinks they're married."

"Did you see him skulking when the giant came for Marlene?" Osbourn said. "What sort of man does that?"

"One with better sense than you and I have," I said, but I felt the same disdain that I heard in Osbourn's voice. Reasonably a man without the training and equipment Osbourn and I had would have committed suicide if he'd gone up against that giant.

But love *wasn't* reasonable, and as a man I couldn't see any comparison between Osbourn and Count Stokes. Further, it seemed to me that Marlene felt the same way about it.

Guntram had gone off with Irene and Osbourn but he came back only now. He walked over to us and said, "Would either of you care to view Master Beddoes's workroom with me? He said you both were welcome to join me."

"Sure," I said. "The things he's showed us already certainly left me interested in seeing more. Are we to go right now?"

"I'm hoping to," said Guntram "But I came back to check with you first."

"Lord Osbourn?"

"I'll let the two of you take the tour," Osbourn said. "I'll stay back here with the boat, if that's all right. I'm not a Maker, after all."

Back with the boat. And with Lady Marlene. "Well, it's fine with me and I doubt Master Beddoes will notice your absence."

"We'll see you when we get back," Guntram said and began leading me toward the Count's palace.

"Let the women know where we've gone if they ask," I called to Osbourn.

They wouldn't ask. In particular Lady Marlene wouldn't ask when she realized that Lord Osbourn was still here.

CHAPTER 13

A Realm of Wonder

We walked to the castle at as brisk a pace as Guntram could manage. He really was in good shape for an old man; but he was an old man.

"Do we need a guide?" I asked Guntram as we approached the entrance archway. The gates had been removed and though there was a slot in the ceiling of the high gatehouse from which a portcullis could fall, the streaks of rust on the stone made it clear that it was rarely—if ever—used. A dozen or so of the sort of folk who gather to watch strangers were doing so here. Four of them were in blue uniforms, but they seemed as mildly interested as the civilians.

"I think I can find the workroom," Guntram said, turning right at a cross corridor. "I visited it when I was here before, though that was just a glance. It's part of the Count's suite on the ground floor."

Civilians drifted about the hall, sometimes talking to one another. At the end of the hallway was a door with an arched entrance where two more guards stood, looking slightly more alert than those at the gate.

"Eakins," Guntram said to the older of the guards. "Master Beddoes invited us to see his collection."

The other guard, a fellow of about my age, stiffened and said, "Well, you better get a pass from the Chamberlain before you expect to go through Lord Stokes's room."

"Rives, don't be a prick," Eakins said. "This is the Maker from Dun Add who was here two weeks ago. If you want to take it up with Stokes that's fine but I'm letting him through."

Rives grimaced and looked at me. "Master Guntram and I are both Makers," I said. "Would you like me to prove that by causing your earring to crawl into your ear instead of hanging from it?"

The guard started back as I hoped he would, reaching up protectively to the simple ring hanging from his left earlobe. It was recently manufactured gold. Not an Ancient artifact. I could with some difficulty separate the ring into a thin gold rod, but I couldn't animate it. The Ancients made metal servitors, but I didn't have that level of skill.

Guntram glanced at me in puzzlement.

Eakins gestured us through the doorway with a smile. Guntram glanced at me but said nothing until we were alone, whereupon he murmured, "I would appreciate it if you taught me that trick."

"If I ever learn to do it I will happily tell you," I said.

Several servants watched us as we walked to another door in the back wall of a sparsely furnished room. It opened promptly at Master Beddoes's pull.

"I saw you were coming," Beddoes said, gesturing with a thin sheet of copper on which a white bead glowed faintly beside a blue one. Lines were scribed on the copper but they were concentric circles rather than a map as I first thought.

"This is only a small thing, of course," he said, waving the sheet again.

"How do you adjust the people it tracks?" Guntram asked. He reached out and waited for Beddoes to give him the artifact. Instead Beddoes turned away and walked deeper into the large hall into which the door opened. It was a busy room with upholstered furniture as well as the shelving and tables piled with artifacts that I'm used to in Makers' workrooms—certainly including my own.

They varied from organized—like Louis's and those of the Makers who worked in his shop to as disorganized as my own and that of Guntram. Organized is clearly better in theory, but though the Makers working for Louis can turn out weapons and shields in quantity very fast—and at the top end (Louis himself) can refine those weapons to channel enormous amounts of energy in a small package, it may take a mind like mine or Guntram's to convert an umbrella into a functioning shield. It wasn't a very good shield, but by the Almighty it was a shield. Only my lack of skill kept me from refining my vision into something more functional.

People differ in outlook. That doesn't mean that Guntram is right or Louis is right. Louis is what the Commonwealth needed to survive. But my sort of mind has been darned useful to the Commonwealth when a large army isn't the best solution.

Though my friends Morseth and Reaves would say brute force was always the *best* way even if other ways might work. As I said, people differ.

"Take a look at this," Beddoes said. He handed me a dozen pebbles strung on nickel wire. I dipped into a trance and found all the pebbles were bits of quartz, occasionally with other elements besides the silicon.

I passed the strand to Guntram, who gave it a similar cursory scan, then returned it to Beddoes when he gestured.

Beddoes fitted a last pebble onto the wire and dangled a string of diamonds from his outstretched index finger. "This is waiting for Lady Marlene when she becomes Countess of Midian," he said proudly.

"That's remarkable!" I said. I reached out for the jewelry. Beddoes hesitated an instant but passed the string over to me. I couldn't detect any difference in the crystals from those of the string of pebbles I'd checked a moment before.

I handed the necklace to Guntram, who asked, "Is there a quicker way to change the jewels than by going into a Maker's trance?"

"It's not possible to change the jewels at all," Beddoes said. "And why would anyone want to? What is more precious than a diamond?"

"The lady might prefer a chain of brilliant rubies," Guntram said mildly. "Depending on what outfit she was wearing."

"That's between her and the Count, it seems to me," Beddoes said, taking the necklace back without ceremony. "It's not a job for a Maker."

Guntram rotated a dull ring he was wearing on his left little finger. The stone was a chip of Blue John, a brittle, bluish-brown stone which could be polished into attractive cups but which had no real value as a gem. I'd never seen it worn as one except this ring of Guntram's.

"Sir?" I said to Beddoes. "Did you prospect the capstone crystal in the Waste yourself?"

"The Waste?" he repeated. "No, that's insanely dangerous! I never go into the Waste. I found this—the capstone as you called it—in a load of streambed gravel being dug for concrete. I saw it through my viewer, much as I did the key that you're carrying. I hope that you've reconsidered and are ready now to sell the key to me so it can be where it belongs?"

"Your viewer has found you some wonderful pieces," I said. "But I think I'll examine the key myself at leisure. After we get back to Dun Add."

Guntram murmured, "May I glance at this for a moment?" and whisked the necklace out of Beddoes's hand. He rubbed the capstone with the Blue John ring.

"Hey, there!" said Beddoes. "What did you do?"

Guntram handed over the necklace. "I touched the capstone with a bit of fluorite, which is much softer than the diamond. The fluorite may have smeared a little on the capstone, but it's unharmed."

"Well, don't do that sort of thing," Beddoes said, turning his back on Guntram. To me he went on, "Now, look at this. It's my real find!"

He pointed to a nondescript ashlar which was covered with pink stucco on one face. "I found this built into the side of a shop on the high street," he said.

I could tell with a quick scan that it was an Ancient artifact, but I hadn't the faintest notion of its purpose.

Beddoes said, "It's a transformer. It converts things into other things of equal mass! Look at this."

He moved a small stack of codices from a nearby table onto a spot directly on front of the indicated block on a larger table. The title of the one on top wasn't on the cover and I couldn't make our what was scribbled on the book's fore-edge. "This is one of the palace cats," Beddoes said. "I changed it last week. It's perfectly all right now as you'll see."

Beddoes touched the block and went into a shallow trance. I glanced at Guntram and found to my surprise that he was in a trance also. I figured he was seeing at a molecular level what

Beddoes was doing. I was more interested in what was happening in Here as I saw it with my own eyes.

The stack of books on the table became a three-colored cat who looked startled, then jumped to the floor and paused to lick her right foreleg. I reached down to rub her with my knuckles. She twisted away at my touch: not angry, but I was a stranger.

"She certainly seems all right," I said, looking up. "That's another unique find, Master Beddoes."

"It is indeed," said Guntram. Then he said, "Look at your necklace, Master Beddoes."

Beddoes was still holding the string in his right hand. It was now of perfectly matched rubies instead of diamonds.

"What!" Beddoes said. Then he snarled at Guntram, "What did you do, you fool?"

"Since the capstone now had the option of projecting corundum rather than merely diamond," Guntram said, "I set it to do that. It can as easily be sapphire if you would prefer that . . . or you can return it to its diamond form."

"Yes, return it, then," Beddoes said. "The diamonds are far superior. And please, Master Guntram, do not meddle in that fashion in the future. I can't say how Count Stokes might respond if he learned what you had done."

"Of course," Guntram said. "What I did was out of place."

He lapsed into a trance again. Guntram certainly had been wrong in choosing that very public method of proving Beddoes was wrong that the stones of the necklace couldn't be changed by a Maker, but Beddoes's assertion of his own exceptional skill was grating—even to me. I could imagine how much more irritating it must be to a Maker as learned as Guntram.

I noticed that Beddoes's workmanship wasn't very good. The viewer that identified Ancient artifacts was a huge find—and the one which made all the others possible. The transformer had been retrieved whole rather than being built up from a scrap the way I'd worked on Beune. The result was extremely good, but it couldn't be duplicated without another viewer. Beddoes was holding a string of diamonds. What Guntram did was repeatable and teachable—I was pretty sure that I could have switched the jewels from rubies to diamonds myself now that I'd been told what was involved. It seemed that was beyond Beddoes's skill. But Beddoes had found the capstone which made the whole operation possible.

"Thank you very much, Master Beddoes," Guntram said. "You truly have remarkable holdings here."

Which he certainly did.

I murmured appreciation, then said, "Sir, is there a way directly into town from here without going out the palace entrance?"

"Why yes," Beddoes said and led us through the hall to a door in the room's sidewall.

"You must realize by now that the key belongs with this collection," he said as he bowed us out.

I nodded and smiled politely, but I didn't speak before we went into a busy street.

"I think Master Beddoes has very modest skills," I said quietly to Guntram as we paused to look at a collection of scarves. I try to bring something home for May when I go off, and a pretty scarf of foreign workmanship was easy to carry. "His viewer is unique and wonderful, though. I wonder what it would have accomplished on Beune?"

"Based on my visits to Beune," Guntram said, "I don't have the impression that the region has a great quantity of Ancient artifacts. The boundary between Here to Not-Here changes fairly frequently on Beune, does it not?"

"Yes," I agreed. "Not in living memory, but if you dig down for a root cellar you can find a layer when Beune was Not-Here. Does that make a difference?"

"It may," said Guntram. Then he said, "Master Beddoes wasn't forced to do low-level work the way I was by my master and you were by lack of an alternative. As a result various things we consider obvious don't leap immediately to his mind."

He paused and added, "Master Beddoes is quite talented, though his attitude makes it hard for me to like him. His lack of practice on low-end work makes it easy to discount his real ability to understand the purpose of large assemblages."

I chose a scarf and said, "Let's get back to the boat and see how Lord Osbourn is getting on."

The shopkeeper was happy to take Commonwealth silver. We went out a gate beside the castle rather than within it.

CHAPTER 14

Coming Down to Cases

When Guntram and I got back, six servants were under a marquee pitched near the boat. They sat on collapsible chairs and six more were set up in the shade of the boat itself where Lord Osbourn and the two women were sitting. They jumped up when they saw us. Lady Irene noted that I was carrying a small packet of the rough cloth in which the huckster had wrapped the scarf I'd bought for May and insisted I show it to her. That wasn't something I'd planned to do and I hesitated.

"I'm not sure I can get it back neat again," I said. "And it's for May."

"I'll rewrap it," Irene said. "Don't you want to see it too, Marlene?"

Marlene nodded and I handed the whole packet to Irene. She had the sacking open as neatly as the shopman had closed it up, then lifted out the scarf. It was really spiderweb thin, and a pale blush that would have vanished against any background less purely white than the skin of Irene's throat against which she held the silk for an instant.

Both women oohed and aahed over the scarf.

"Your wife is very fortunate, Lord Pal," Marlene said. She refolded the cloth herself before handing it to Irene, who returned it to me.

"They do very fine lace here on Midian," I explained. "The color is from the cocoon itself, the way the worm spun it. I hope May will like it."

I cleared my throat and added, "Ah, Lady May and I are together for the rest of my life I hope, but we're not married. It's customary for the Consort's ladies in waiting to remain single, and May didn't want marriage."

"It's a protection for the woman," said Lady Irene.

"She'll have whatever she tells me she wants," I said, a little angry now. I hated to think that May felt she needed protection from the way I was going to treat her, but if she did, she did. I wasn't happy with a discourteous third party implying that May did, though.

"Lord Pal?" Osbourn said, maybe to change the subject. "Could you go back in the city and show me around? I'll like to have a meal that doesn't come out of the converter. It always tastes fine, but I'd like a real sausage, you know."

"Sure," I said. "Let me put this away and I'll be right out."

Each compartment in the boat had drawers built into its base. As usual, I was carrying only an extra suit for dress, the same as I'd have done if Baga and I were on foot. I set the scarf beside the suit and came back outside.

"You all going to be all right?" I asked the women.

"Of course," said Irene, which was pretty much what I thought as well, but it seemed like the polite thing to do before we went. Besides the local servants, a dozen Midian guards were between the boat and the empty enclosure.

"I wonder what they think they'll be able to do if another giant comes out of the Waste?" Lord Osbourn said.

"Well, they killed the shrew that came out earlier," I said. "And anyway, now that Lady Marlene's been released maybe there won't be any more drawn to this place. There were sure questions I'd have liked to ask Master Hector if he hadn't been pointlessly killed."

We reached the gate in the city wall that Guntram and I had come out of. "You're looking for sausage?" I said.

"To tell the truth," said Osbourn, "what I'd really like to do is to get lace like you did, but for Marlene. Do you suppose they'd have a blue to match her eyes?"

"I haven't looked at Marlene that carefully," I said, wondering how easy it was going to be to work backward into Midian. "I don't think I'm going to. And you really shouldn't either, Osbourn. Not while we're still on Midian."

With the back wall of the palace on my left it really wasn't hard to find my way back to the shop where I'd been before. The shopkeeper was delighted; apparently the nearby jeweler had told him that the silver Riders I'd paid him were nineteen parts pure rather than eleven in twelve as was standard in Midian. Osbourn settled on a rather larger scarf than I had gotten, of a blue that he found satisfactory.

When he'd finished we went back into the street. "If you're not in too much of a hurry to get back to Marlene," I said, "there's a decent-looking restaurant just down the block here. Want to try that?"

In truth, Osbourn had gotten me thinking about real food which hadn't been processed through a converter. We had a meal of sausage and beer for me and red wine for Osbourn. The sausage was a touch greasy and the lager was fixed with something more bitter than I was used to, but withal it was a wonderful change from the pureed sameness of what we would have gotten aboard the boat.

I was having a second beer while Osbourn finished his bottle of wine. A woman came over to the table exchanging occasional friendly words with waiters as she passed through. She turned a chair from a nearby table and sat between us. She said, "Greshan the goldsmith says you're from the Commonwealth. Maybe as strangers you'd like a guide around Midian? My name's Diane."

I was trying to frame a polite way of sending her off, but before I could speak, Lord Osbourn sneered, "Not of your sort, trollop."

Diane drew herself up stiffly. Her dark blue dress was of a hard fabric that wasn't silk; a processed cotton, I supposed. It struck me that the scarf Osbourn had just bought would be a perfect complement to it.

"That's not very friendly for a total stranger," she said. "You folks looked like men, but maybe you're queer for each other? Is that it?"

"I won't bandy words with your like!" Lord Osbourn replied, bandying words pointlessly.

The woman was already standing up. I laid a hand on Osbourn's shoulder to keep him seated. "I'm sorry, Diane, we've had a long voyage and we're very tired." I laid a polished brass Fiver on the table and said, "Have a drink on us. Lord Osbourn, let's get back to the ladies. They'll be worried."

We went out into the street with no further incidents. Lord Osbourn growled, "She honestly expected me to be interested in her!"

"She wasn't bad looking," I said, trying to keep things calm. I was surprised that Osbourn, usually even tempered, had gotten abusively angry. Maybe it was the suggestion that he and I were lovers, though he'd been pretty hostile to her from the first.

"Marlene's a lot prettier," Osbourn said. "And she's got brains besides."

We reached the gate in the wall again. "We don't know anything important about Diane," I said. "Except that Count Stokes doesn't think they're married."

Guntram was outside with the women when we arrived at the boat. They greeted us warmly and for a moment I was afraid Lady Marlene was going to throw her arms around Osbourn. I'd have intervened if that happened, and though I didn't have to, I sure wasn't looking forward to the interview with Count Stokes when Marlene announced her decision.

In the morning, I took Sam out on the Road. We had nowhere to go, but it gets old sitting in the boat and Sam needed a jaunt as badly as I did.

I didn't wake Lord Osbourn as he liked to sleep later than I did, and I knew he'd been awake chatting with Lady Marlene until the small hours of the morning. It wasn't my place to object, but I'd surely rather they displayed more decorum while we were in Count Stokes's domains.

Christiana might have liked to go with us but I refused to take her. She was Osbourn's dog and she shouldn't get into the habit of working with somebody else. A warrior and his dog had to have a perfect bond or the result in a fight was likely to be fatal.

We went up the Road to the next landingplace. I would generally have checked about the neighborhood with the Clerk of Here before I went off on a patrol, but because I was going by boat this time I hadn't bothered to. I suspected that they were administered by Midian.

I didn't go into the node I'd reached, just turned around and went back to Midian. Visiting unfamiliar nodes was still exciting to me after being raised on Beune, which was a long way from places that anybody would want to be, but right at the moment my attention was on the political situation if Lady Marlene decided not to go through with her marriage with the Count. We'd wait out the week, but the decision was pretty obvious already.

I wondered what would have happened if Lord Osbourn hadn't come along. The giant coming out of the Waste just then had been chance, but even without that striking illustration of the difference between Osbourn and the Count my companion would have ranked pretty high. He was handsome, smart and the same apparent age as Lady Marlene because the years in Master Hector's prison hadn't weighed on Marlene the same way they had on those outside. Like Count Stokes.

The situation might cause problems for the Leader. I didn't doubt that Jon would back me, but he might wish that I'd convinced Osbourn to think again about the situation. I was pretty sure Osbourn had been thinking about the lady much more frequently than that.

Sam and I returned to Midian at a more leisurely pace than we'd gone out.

The point at which the node of Midian impinged on the Road—landingplace—was much broader than most. You could have driven an oxcart onto it without brushing the Waste to either side—if you could have gotten an ox or any other herbivore onto the Road without it panicking.

Sam and I headed straight for the boat expecting to relax. To my surprise Christiana was barking furiously on the ground and Irene was coming out of the hatch shouting, "Come on, then!"

The palace servants had vanished. More to my surprise the platoon of uniformed guards had moved off also. There wasn't anything they could really do against another giant, but as I'd said to Osbourn there were more monsters than that in the Waste.

Sam was getting excited also from Christiana's barking. Lord Osbourn came out of the hatch, adjusting the bandolier from which his shield and weapon hung. "I'm ready!" he shouted back to Irene. Then he saw me and said, "Lord Pal! Where were you? Will you back me?"

"Yes," I said, because that's the right answer any time a friend asks you for help. "But what in the name of heaven is going on?"

"Stokes's brutes have kidnapped Marlene!" Lady Irene said. "We'd gone back to the enclosure to get a rhododendron in a pot that Marlene wanted to take with her to Dun Add—she's not staying on Midian. But when we started to come out one of the Count's clerks came in with the soldiers and they took Marlene into the palace. I came back here and woke up Lord Osbourn. I didn't know where you were!"

"I'm here now," I said, keeping my voice calm and not reacting to Lady Irene's obvious anger at me for not having checked in with her before I got some exercise. To Osbourn I said, "Have you talked to anybody yet?"

"I just woke up," Lord Osbourn said. "I guess we have to, don't we? I'm so angry that I'd probably say the wrong thing if I tried, so you'd better do the talking, Pal."

"The time for talking was before they stole off a girl they knew was under our protection," I said. "I'll lead, sure, but I don't think we're going to talk very much."

I nodded to the main gate of the palace no longer a real fortress, thank goodness. I took out my equipment.

"Come on, Sam," I said as I switched my weapon on and went up a plane on which the normal aspects of Here and humans without Ancient hardware were ghostly shadows. "We're going calling on the neighbors."

Lord Osbourn took my left side, five feet distant so that we wouldn't get in one another's way, as we headed for the entrance. By the time we were halfway there, a fellow in a flowing robe stepped out flanked by at least fifteen of Lord Stokes's guards. They were all armed, and they switched on as we approached. They didn't have dogs, though, which would make them much less agile than me and Osbourn in a fight.

The fellow in the robe was speaking but he wasn't shouting loudly enough for me to understand him with my weapon on. I switched off and called, "We have come for Lady Marlene, who is under my protection. Will you surrender her without violence?"

The clerk—that was what Irene had called him and it seemed likely enough—shouted back, "Count Stokes will not turn over his wife to foreign adventurers! Go away or it will be worse for you!"

He must have given a signal to the guards, because the blue-uniformed squad stepped forward in a wobbly line. I was glad now that Tsetzas had already been killed. I'd liked and respected him, the more so after his suicidal rush at the giant. He'd have done the same thing with me—and would have died just as surely:

liking the man wouldn't have prevented me from doing my duty to get Lady Marlene back.

I had the lead in this, partly because I was afraid that Osbourn might have hesitation about what we were doing. I didn't. I'd committed and that was it.

The second man from my right in the line was slightly ahead of the guards to either side of him. As I suspected, he paused to look to his side when he realized he was getting ahead. I didn't need his momentary inattention to take him but I used it, lunging forward to thrust past the angle of his shield and stab him through the top of his chest. He toppled backward, drawing the attention of the guy on his right he'd been looking at.

I thrust through the center of that man's shield. I started to say "without art" but in fact I was making the point of how much better my weapon was than the shields of most of these guards. I was willing to kill all the Count's men, but I'd rather frighten them into running away.

Sam and I went through the gap in the line. I almost collided with the clerk, screaming in terror and stumbling headlong as he tried to get away. Sam and I turned. If the sprawled clerk had been armed, I'd have killed him; but as it was, even behind me he was no threat.

I took a guard through the hip from behind. He toppled, and Osbourn, coming through the line, hacked down the man beside him.

Osborn and I stood together with the surviving guards facing us in a clump, none of them between us and the gateway. Osbourn and I couldn't communicate with our weapons on but he knew to back me as I charged the guards. My purpose was to do as much damage as possible to prevent them from following us into the palace.

One guard met me with a thrust which I took on my shield. Before he could withdraw his arm I'd severed it and his weapon thumped to the ground. Three rushed together from my left. They were getting in their own way from the beginning, but the confusion got worse after Osbourn thrust the outside man through the knee and he sprawled in front of his fellows. I stabbed quickly.

Lord Osbourn and I were working as a team; without coordination, numbers are a handicap.

There were still five or six guards upright, but they were the men who'd hung back earlier in the fighting. I was breathing hard and really wanted this business to be over. I swung toward the guards, advancing my shield. Osbourn was beside me.

One man bolted; then they all scattered back across landingplace. I switched off and looked around. My equipment was only vaguely warm from the work it had done. There was a nice breeze but the air in the gateway was thick with the stench of blood and the wastes men had voided as they died. The sharpness of ozone cut through other smells.

I turned to the clerk and said, "Lead us to Lady Marlene!"

"I'm not sure!" the clerk said. "I didn't see her after she went inside!"

Lord Osbourn switched his weapon back on and took a step toward the clerk. The clerk shouted, "I'll see!" and scrambled through the palace gateway. Lord Osbourn may not have been able to understand the words, but he wasn't hot tempered and I wasn't worried that he was going to cut the civilian down. I ran along with them. There was a chance that an archer was going to pot me since my equipment was off, but I decided being able to see and hear normally was worth the risk.

The clerk shouted to a servant lurking in an alcove half the length of the room away. I thought for a moment that fellow wasn't going to respond but as I started toward him he pointed toward the back of the room where I knew the door to Master Beddoes's quarters was.

The pair of guards were gone but Count Stokes himself stepped into the inner doorway. He carried a shield and weapon of excellent quality. "Count Stokes!" I cried. "We've come for Lady Marlene. If you hand her over we'll go away and not trouble you further. You won't be harmed."

"You're bandits and I can't trust you!" Stokes said. "You're just the sort of bride stealers as Master Hector was. I'll protect Lady Marlene from you or die trying!"

This was awkward. I didn't see any way to rescue Marlene that didn't involve going through Stokes, and the incident even if told with an attempt at neutrality was going to look like a particularly brutal piece of bride theft. I hadn't expected the Count to show so much backbone.

Lord Osbourn had also switched off his equipment. He looked

around. The clerk was close behind us. Osbourn pointed to him and said, "You! Servant! You're my witness!"

"I am Treasurer Keames," the clerk said. "What am I witnessing?"

Osbourn turned to Stokes. "Your lordship!" he shouted. "I challenge you to fight me man to man for Lady Marlene! Lord Pal—" he turned to me "—swear on your honor as a Champion that you will abide by this arrangement—and not interfere with the duel or with Count Stokes if he defeats me."

Lord Osbourn couldn't commit me—and he knew that—but under the circumstances I was willing to be bound. "I swear!" I said. "If Count Stokes defeats you, I go back to Dun Add and Lady Marlene remains here with her husband!"

"You can't do that!" Lady Irene cried. "You can't turn Marlene over to that old brute!"

"Lady Irene," I said, "I don't take orders from you. I will support the decision of my friend and colleague."

Irene's interference underlined her basic overestimate of her own importance, but it was the perfect goad to bring Stokes to an irrevocable decision. "I accept your terms, Lord Pal!" he said and switched on his shield and weapon. He attacked Osbourn at once.

Those were Osbourn's terms, not mine. I was only willing to accept them because I knew that the Count didn't have a prayer of winning a duel with Lord Osbourn. Their equipment was comparable, but Osbourn had Champion's training and recent practice. Count Stokes had arrogance and probably an inflated sense of his own skill.

He struck an overhead blow which would probably have crashed through the shield of most opponents to be met this far from Dun Add. Osbourn's weapon guided the stroke into the floor where it crackled and burned though the marble slabs. Stokes really did have a powerful weapon, even better than I'd thought at a quick glance.

From experience I knew that even redirecting a blow like that could be a numbing experience. Osbourn responded quickly, striking sideways at Stokes's abdomen. Stokes blocked the blow easily with his shield but it kept him off-balance.

Stokes had to struggle to withdraw his weapon from the stone floor. When it came he lurched backward. Osbourn had been waiting for that and hacked off Stokes's right foot while his shield was hopelessly out of position.

Stokes flailed wildly with his weapon as he fell backward onto his left side. He was still dangerous, just as the giant had been. Stokes rose onto his knees with his left hand, trying to lift his torso from the floor instead of advancing the shield.

Lord Osbourn stepped in, using his shield to block the swipes of Stokes's weapon. Then he stabbed down with clinical precision, through the Count's collarbone and into his chest cavity. Stokes collapsed onto his face.

Osbourn stepped back and switched off his weapon and shield.

I turned and said, "Sir! Treasurer! What did you just see?"

A dozen people besides Irene and Treasurer Keames had by now entered the large entrance hall, though I wasn't sure that most of them could hear Keames when he said, "The warrior from Dun Add challenged Count Stokes. Count Stokes attacked him. The warrior from Dun Add defeated the Count."

"Go out and tell everyone you meet what you just saw," I said loudly. "The warrior is Lord Osbourn of Madringor. And now, Osbourn, let's go into Master Beddoes's domain and free Lady Marlene. That's what we came to Midian to do, after all."

"Greetings, your lordships," Master Beddoes said, stepping out from behind a couch that probably doubled as a place to sleep.

"We're here to free Lady Marlene," I said. "Where is she?"

The room was the same untidy jumble of furniture, books and artifacts that I'd seen before. Guntram and Lady Irene had entered behind Osbourn and me. The Count's corpse in the doorway seemed to have blocked any potential spectators.

"Count Stokes brought the lady here by force," Beddoes said. "She wasn't injured but he threatened her with his weapon."

"Where is she?" Lord Osbourn demanded.

Beddoes turned from Osbourn to me and said, "I'll trade her to you, Lord Pal. In exchange for the key you have no use for."

"By the Almighty!" Osbourn shouted. "I've killed five men today! Do you think I'll hesitate at a sixth?"

The frame that displayed Ancient artifacts was indeed a wonderful device. But in a sense, what Louis or Guntram—or me a tiny way—did was more wonderful, in teasing out the purposes the Ancients had built into artifacts which had been worn to pebbles; and in the case of Louis, sometimes improving the device beyond what it originally had been, because he understood the principles which underlay the operation.

Stokes had forgotten he was dealing with the honor of the Commonwealth, not just a couple of wandering warriors. He was—had been—a very big man on Midian, and he thought that made him bigger in the wider world than perhaps he should have.

I said, "Lord Osbourn, I never want to consider killing a man because I find it the simplest answer to a problem. It certainly may be the correct answer, but not just the simplest."

I took the key out of my purse and handed it to Beddoes. "I'd appreciate learning how it works," I said. "But that's not required. Marlene's safe return in."

"Of course," Beddoes said, nodding. He sidled over to his converter and paused beside a stack of codices on top of a large table. He reached over to the converter and went into a light trance. The pile of books on the table shifted into Marlene. She was on the edge and would have fallen off if Lord Osbourn hadn't leaped to that point and caught her.

Osbourn straightened. He didn't push Marlene away, but the sudden rigidity of his body caused her to twitch apart from him in surprise.

"Lord Pal," he said. "I misspoke. Please forgive me."

"You've shown exceptional judgment as well as skill this morning," I said. "This confirms the high opinion of you which the Leader and I share."

Master Beddoes cleared his throat for attention. When I looked toward him, he said, "You asked how the key works, your lordship." He held it out toward me. "I suggest that you or Master Guntram demonstrate it yourself."

"Where do you suggest we do that?" I asked calmly. Beddoes had something in mind, but I was hanged if I could see what it was.

Beddoes held out the key to me. "Anywhere there's a door," he said. He gestured toward the door at the back which I knew led to the alley. "That one over there's probably the closest."

I took the key and went to the door. I tried it and found it locked as I expected. The keyhole was an ordinary one. "This key won't fit," I said, looking over my shoulder toward Beddoes.

"Try it," he said and I did. The hollow key entered the opening, though I was sure that it was too thick to enter the hole for the key shaft. I successfully tried to turn it and felt something engage. I used the key itself as a handle and pulled the panel open. Instead of the alley and passing citizens, the room beyond reminded me of Master Sans's Underworld as Lady Irene and I had seen it.

The furnishings were sparkling crystal, probably diamond as those of the Underworld had been. On the tops and shelves were bales of fabric and devices for purposes I couldn't for the most part even guess at.

I recognized a frame like the one which Beddoes used to identify Ancient artifacts, however. I thought it very likely that more of the hundreds of devices were of similar value.

I stepped into the area beyond the door. It wasn't a room or an enclosure of any type. On all sides but that of the doorway by which I'd entered, it was a bubble in the Waste. Even without touching the artifacts, I could sense their power. This was the most remarkable place I'd ever seen.

I wanted to get out. I've spent many hours prospecting in the Waste. I'm not afraid of it: just careful. This was unfamiliar and therefore frightening.

I started to back out and collided with Guntram. "No!" I said. "Get out of here!"

I resumed backing but didn't turn my head until I saw from the corners of my eyes that I was back in Beddoes's workroom. I sighed with relief.

"What's wrong?" asked Guntram, who'd skipped back out as I'd ordered.

I took another deep breath and muttered, "I'm not sure. I didn't like the way it felt. I remembered Master Sans being eaten by a thing from the Waste when he was caught in the open. That whole room, *place*, is open."

Lady Irene, carrying her bundle of yarrow stalks, stepped around me and Guntram. I couldn't have stopped her and didn't see any reason to try. She looked around the alcove in the Waste, lifted and shook out with her free hand a swatch of fabric which seemed to have a rose embroidered on it, then set it down again. She came back out.

"The key makes that magic with your sticks unnecessary," Beddoes said. He took out the key and waggled it at Irene, then nodded toward me.

Beddoes glowered at her, then walked into the alcove himself, holding the key ostentatiously up in his right hand. He first looked at the frame that I'd noticed on the nearest shelf. He looked back at me and said, "Lord Pal, superstition has cost you a great deal."

"Your instincts have proved good in the past," Guntram said quietly to me. "You're correct to trust them now."

"Thank you, friend," I said. "I've gotten along thus far, and getting rich has never been a goal."

Lady Irene slammed the alley door closed. The alcove in which Beddoes stood vanished.

"He made a point of keeping the key with him," I said. Beddoes wasn't likeable, but the place he'd gone into had bothered me just to be in. He didn't deserve to be abandoned there—even if it had been possible to get him out.

Of course if I'd been a woman who'd been badly treated by most of the men in her life, I might feel more harshly than I did about the kidnapping of Lady Marlene.

"Yes," Irene said. "Master Beddoes can open a door to somewhere. But not, I hope, back to here."

"In my brief glimpse of the place he went into," Guntram said, "I didn't see a door. Did you, Lord Pal?"

"I didn't," I said. The drawbolt on the alley door was still closed in its staples on the jamb, despite my having opened it moments before. I slid the bolt open and raised the latch, then tugged the panel open normally. The pair of men passing by in the alley glanced at me on their way into a tavern whose swinging door closed behind them.

I banged the panel shut again, looked back to find my companions, even Irene, staring intently at me. I jerked the door open. The alley was still outside. I closed and latched the door.

"Maybe Beddoes understands what's happening," I said to Guntram. "He knew about the key already before he met me. He'd read about it somewhere."

"I doubt he knew very much," Guntram said. "By taking the key with him he prevented us from opening the door to rescue him."

"He used my friend Marlene to bargain with!" Lady Irene said. "I didn't mean to kill him, but I don't care if he dies."

Osbourn and Marlene came closer when they heard her name. I looked at them and said, "I guess I don't care either. But—"

I thought of the wizened corpse I'd ordered to be buried on Winslow, having pried the shrunken fingers of his right hand open to take the key. I hadn't been able to guess why he'd died with it in the Waste. Now I wondered if a closing door had left him in the middle of the Waste with an enormous treasure of Ancient artifacts, but no way to return to Here. That alcove might not have been a deliberate trap; but it was surely a trap nonetheless.

"I'd rather he hadn't died that particular way, though. But it's too late to worry about now."

I opened the alley door again and stepped out of the palace. I was in the way of folk walking through the tight space. I just wanted to be out of the building, though I knew that the opening onto the Waste wasn't really part of the palace.

After a time, Guntram called from the doorway saying, "Pal, what should we do next?"

I opened my eyes and turned from the coarse brick wall of the building behind the palace. My hands were gritty from pressing against the wall. I rubbed them together, then crossed back into the palace during a break in the sporadic traffic.

"Next," I said, "you and I, my friend, will sort through Master Beddoes's workroom and decide what we're going carry back to Dun Add with us. I very much doubt Master Beddoes will be returning, and if he does we'll have kept his artifacts safe for him."

CHAPTER 15

Back in Dun Add

While we were on Midian the local problems were the only thing on my mind, but as we neared Dun Add I kept thinking about Lady Hope and her sister. Irene was interested only in what was happening at her school while she was absent and took her bundle of yarrow stalks straight back to that property. As for me, I left Baga and Guntram to sort out the contents of the boat and went straight to Lady Jolene's suite.

There were two Champions present, neither of whom I knew well: Lord Trapson and Efrit of Steinholm. Trapson was sitting with Lady Beatrice. They'd known one another before coming to Dun Add and had gotten to know each other better here. For the most part the ladies in waiting didn't pay a lot of attention to matters outside their personal orbit, but one asked as I was kissing Lady May in greeting, "Were you able to free the imprisoned bride?"

"Lady Marlene is free," I said, "and probably married to Lord Osbourn of Madringor by now. But speaking of women in distress, do any of you know how the lawsuit over the Count of Laferriere's will has gone?"

I thought Lady Beatrice might respond but unexpectedly the Consort herself volunteered, "Jon mentioned that the Council of Five is to deliver its judgment this morning. It's still before noon, isn't it?" She turned to see where the light through the Oriel window was falling. "Yes, you've still got time, Lord Pal. If you want to go."

In truth I did, but I checked with May and only when she shrugged did I say, "I think I will run down to the court and see that it's taken care of."

The auditorium could be entered on three levels, but the top was the ordinary access for spectators, which is all I was. I went down to that end of the corridor and the ushers nodded me through the entrance. I took a seat to the side three rows down, low enough down to avoid any chatter in the hall.

The leader in the center of the facing wall said, "Is the secretary of the Council of Five ready to announce a judgment in the matter of the Count of Laferriere's will?"

He didn't shout, but the court's acoustics were so good that everyone in the room could hear him.

"We are, your lordship," said Lady Noonen, a wizened woman and a noted legal scholar said. She was seated directly below Jon, facing the sisters and the clerks acting for them. "Will the parties please rise?" a steward beside Noonen said.

The sisters, on opposite sides of the ground level, rose. I had a better view of Joy on the opposite side than I did of Hope directly below me. Joy was a lush blond, seated between two clerks whom I recognized as living in Dun Add, though I didn't recall their names.

"The unanimous judgment of the council is in favor of Lady Hope of Laferriere," Noonen said. "The council will appoint commissioners to divide the decedent's property equally between the parties."

There was no outcry, but Lady Hope bent to hug Mistress Loong's shoulders. A local clerk, Master Toshi, was seated on her other side. Lady Joy sat down and one of her clerks hopped to his feet and announced, "Lady Joy of Laferriere asserts her right of appeal to combat."

"Noted," said Lady Noonen, as she made a notation on the tablet before her.

I got to my feet and walked down the side aisle to where Lady Hope sat with her legal team. Master Toshi was speaking to Hope and Loong, probably explaining appeal to combat to visitors not familiar with Commonwealth practice.

Toshi stopped and looked up at me. "Milord?" he said, calling the attention of the two women to me. They looked over at me.

"I just came over to offer my services as a Champion," I said. "If Lady Hope hasn't already engaged someone, that is."

"Lord Pal!" said Toshi reverently. "I saw you defeat Lord Baran!"

"I don't understand," Hope said. "You are a clerk, Lord Pal? I thought you were a Maker."

"I'm not a clerk," I said. "But I'm a specialist in the kind of law you need right now. Master Toshi will explain the details to you. But you may want to get other representation."

I turned and walked back up the aisle toward the door I'd come in by. I really hadn't meant to do that, but it was the right decision.

"She accepts if she's sane, Lord Pal," Master Toshi called after me.

I went directly back to Jolene's suite to tell May. I didn't know how she was going to take it since I hadn't mentioned what I was planning. I *wasn't* planning it.

The Council of Five had looked at the evidence and come to a decision. Lady Joy decided she wouldn't accept the decision and was appealing to force, which was within the law—but wasn't right, in my opinion. If she wanted force she'd get it.

One of the guards in the corridor called, "Lord Pal's back already," and the door opened immediately from the inside guard pushing it. May was beside him and kissed me firmly before guiding me into the suite. To the assembly I said, "the council found for Lady Hope. Lady Joy immediately appealed to combat. I volunteered to Lady Hope that I would represent her if she wished. I hadn't expected this result and I acted without discussing the matter with anyone, including my friend Lady May."

I dipped my head to her in apology. "You did the right thing, Pal," she said, to my relief. "As you usually do. You couldn't let a nice lady be robbed."

Lord Trapson said, "Who's your opponent, Lord Pal?"

"I don't know," I said. "I don't really care. The clerk didn't say, though they must've had something in mind since they were prepared to appeal as soon as the verdict was announced."

That made me think about my challenge as leading to a real fight, which I hadn't done when I made it. When I fought on behalf of Lady Jolene no member of the Hall of Champions would stand with me. Jolene wasn't guilty of poisoning Lord Baran's friend, but she certainly was having an affair with Lord Clain. With Clain far from Dun Add—but nobody knew exactly where—only an outsider like me would take Jolene's cause, and no warrior would back me. Makers from Master Louis's shop brought me water and sponged my arm overheated from holding my weapon while I fought the stronger man.

Now I was a significant player in Dun Add. There were no political limitations on this combat. I could ask any warrior in Dun Add to stand on the sidelines and coach me.

My two closest friends among the Champions were Morseth and Reaves. I decided I would ask one of them at my earliest opportunity.

The door opened to admit one of Jon's personal couriers, who went immediately to kneel beside the Consort and whisper in her ear.

He rose to leave. Jolene unexpectedly got to her feet and said, "Lord Trapson raised a question and now there's an answer. Lady Joy of Laferriere has named Lord Morseth as Champion for her appeal of the Council of Five's judgment."

Lady May was holding my arm. Her grip suddenly tightened hard.

My chest tightened also. May noticed my expression and said, "Are you all right, Pal? Morseth is a potent warrior. Do you doubt you can beat him?"

"I can beat him," I said. "Only, a part of me isn't sure I want to."

Before I left Jolene's suite I took May aside and murmured to her, "I won't be going straight home, love. I want to stop at Lord Morseth's house and chat with him."

"Would you like me to come along with you?" May said, looking at me with fixed determination.

"No," I said, trying to keep my tone light. "We're just going to chat."

May had been friends with Morseth—and Reaves—from before I'd come to Dun Add. I'd never asked how *well* they'd known one another. It was none of my business.

I did know that Morseth had never been a man to ignore a pretty girl, and there were very few girls prettier than May.

May's presence at a meeting between me and Morseth would have added a level of tension. I didn't want to risk a bad result.

Our townhouse was on South Street. Morseth and his friend Reaves were across the street from one another two blocks to the west. A doorman I didn't recognize let me in and I found Reaves already talking with Morseth.

Morseth jumped up when he saw me. "Pal!" he called. "Lord knows I didn't expect you'd be fighting for Lady Hope! How do you know her?"

"I don't, really," I said. The friends had been drinking wine when I came in. The servant brought in a third glass and filled it for me. I took a sip, but I don't like wine and this was a strong vintage. Me getting drunk wouldn't make the discussion easier.

"May brought her over to fix her broach that her sister Joy had scratched. It's an Ancient artifact, and I fixed it."

"If you don't really know her..." Morseth said. "Maybe we can work something out. I sure don't want to fight you, buddy."

"And I don't want to fight *you*, Morseth," I said. "I'm in this for justice, same as I was when Lord Baran went after the Consort. You remember that, Morseth. A lot of better qualified people wouldn't stand up for her because they thought she was having an affair with Lord Clain."

"She *was* having an affair!" Reaves said.

"Sure she was!" I said, sipping enough wine to cut the dryness of my mouth.

"I didn't like how Jolene and Clain were carrying on," I said. My voice was rising despite me. "We aren't sophisticated people on Beune. But I thought justice was more important than somebody's private life. And I still think that!"

CHAPTER 16

Preparation for Combat

I was really wrung out when I got home at midday after hours of sparring. May drew me a large mug of ale before I sat down, and said, "I hope it's gone better than you look."

"It hasn't," I said. "Morseth is going to kill me. Literally. Sure as sunrise."

May sat down on the bench close to me. She leaned her breast onto my left biceps. "Morseth's your friend," she said. "He doesn't want to kill you."

"He's Lady Joy's Champion," I said. "I'm Hope's Champion. I've never known Morseth to go less than full house in fighting a battle."

"Do you think there's anything I can do?" May said.

I stopped myself before I blurted, "Go to Morseth and beg him to spare me?" I wasn't willing for that to happen—and it wouldn't make any difference. Morseth was a friend of May's but that wasn't going to stop him from doing his job.

"Go to a temple and pray," I said instead. "I doubt it will do much good, but I doubt anything will."

"Dear," May said, "I'm not willing to write you off yet." She leaned over and kissed me. "You beat Lord Baran, after all."

Listening to somebody positive really did make me feel better.

"Morseth is probably better than Baran was," I said. I was thinking now rather than just reacting gloomily. "And Baran didn't take me seriously. Morseth will."

"Can you wear him down?" May asked. "The way you did Baran?"

We kissed again. My hands were fondling her bodice. I was definitely feeling better. "I didn't really wear Baran down," I said. "He just got impatient. Morseth's too smart for that to work with him."

Morseth was *very* smart. He'd made an able replacement for Lord Clain when Clain visited his distant holdings in order to let the talk about him and Jolene cool off. Letting the talk die down was the Commonwealth's best available option, because the couple themselves weren't going to cool down if they were on the same node.

I don't know how Jon felt about it. That was nothing I'd discuss with him or with any other man. I'd heard folks say that Jon couldn't afford to get crossways with a warrior as important to the Commonwealth as Clain was. I'm not sophisticated, but I've seen enough of Jon to doubt that being afraid would have kept him from doing any bloody thing if he wanted to do it.

He surely cared for Jolene—and for Clain too; they were friends. It wouldn't have gone over well in Beune, but I'd learned when I first came to Dun Add that what was true in Beune didn't always hold for the rest of the universe.

I didn't like it but I'm not the Almighty. My mom may have thought she spoke for Him when she talked about right and wrong, but I never believed that even when I pretty much followed her rules for myself.

"I know you, Pal," May said. "You'll think of something."

"I've thought of something," I said. "But I'm not willing to cripple my friend Morseth."

"Not even if it means he kills you?" she said, getting back to the same place as Clain had.

"That's on Morseth!" I said. "What he's got to live with for the rest of *his* life."

There wasn't much way you could end a real fight without at least one party being dead or crippled. Not with full-power weapons. I'd gotten out of my first fight just bruised because Guntram had dropped both parties into blackness, but that couldn't happen in a judicial duel like this.

"Unless Joy is suddenly struck by sisterly affection, and that's not going to happen," I said, "the fight isn't going to end in a good way."

I started wondering if I'd be willing to cut Morseth's foot off when I came down to cases. His foot or my life. I hoped I wouldn't decide to do that, but I'm not always the man I wish I were. Might Jon stop the combat because Morseth and I were both important to the Commonwealth?

No, because justice under the laws was even more important to him. If you change the laws when you don't like the result, that's not the sort of impartial justice that people believe in at the core of their beings. For that you need justice that doesn't change.

"Maybe the Almighty will intervene to change Joy's mind," May said, starting to tug me upstairs to the bedroom. That was usually her response to a difficult situation, and a pretty good one.

I was going to miss living with her a lot.

CHAPTER 17

Preparations

The next morning I was about to go to the practice hall to meet Guntram again when May said, "Come back home at noon, will you? We'll have lunch together and I hope to have a friend in."

"Sure," I said. "I'd be better off with a break then anyway."

Another time I'd have argued that I wasn't in a mood for company—which was more true than not any day of my life. But it was something May wanted and I didn't feel like saying no to her about anything right at the moment. Anyway, a break was a good idea.

I started thinking about wearing Morseth down. I didn't think I could do it, but apart from divine intervention, it was the best chance I had if I wasn't willing to trick him and cut his foot off.

I didn't know what the real difference was between a trick, and me getting home with a thrust because Lord Morseth got tired and sloppy. The wound had to be serious enough to end the fight, and weapons did a great deal of damage at full power.

I'd always done what I thought was right, whether or not I had cold reason on my side. Reason can trick you. My gut never had.

I was in the practice hall when a courier summoned me to come to Jolene's suite at midday. My first thought of course was that something had happened to May, but it was midmorning, still two hours short of noon, so this wasn't an emergency. I told Guntram I'd run two more jousts and then had to go off for a meeting. I had no idea what the Consort might want me for and I didn't like mysteries, but it wasn't my place to question her.

I didn't go home to change clothes but I did take a shower after the second bout. Since I'd begun living with May I always dressed presentably if not in the highest fashion. When I first came to Dun Add I dressed for work as I had as a peasant.

May felt that was impolite when I was meeting important people. I didn't see how that could be, but Mom had raised me to be polite and May knew a lot more about important people than I did. In any case so long as quality clothes were cut loosely I could fight in them as well as I could in the shirt and breeches I'd wear for plowing.

"Ma'am?" I said when I was ushered into the suite. Nothing unusual was going on. Lord Trent, a recent Champion, was present beside the Consort and half a dozen ladies in waiting.

Jolene said, "Come, Pal. I need you at a discussion. It won't take long."

The back entrance to the Leader's sanctum was guarded by a Champion named Monroe. Not one of my friends, but a skilled warrior and certainly to be trusted to keep unauthorized people away from Jon.

Jolene opened the inner door without knocking. Clain was sitting across Jon's small desk from him. Both men jumped up when they saw us but Jolene waved them back down.

"I brought Lord Pal up so that all three of you understand what I'm doing," she said. I stood in the doorway for lack of space in the private office. That meant the door could be closed but if anybody cared they could move the meeting to somewhere else.

"Pal represented me when Lord Baran accused me of poisoning his friend Lord Gismonde," Jolene continued. Both men remembered very well, though Clain had been absent from Dun Add when it happened.

"At the time I thought it would be improper for him to wear my favor during the duel, because I'm the Leader's Consort," Jolene said. "And frankly I was angry to be put in such a position. I thought Pal would certainly lose and Baran would have me boiled in oil as his intention very publicly was. Pal, I apologize."

"Milady, I didn't think I could intervene without irreparable harm to the Commonwealth!" Jon said.

"And I was on the eastern Marches and had no idea of what

was going on in Dun Add!" Clain said. "You know I'd have been back at once if I had known. I was back as soon as I learned."

"Yes, that's certainly true," Jolene agreed. "Lord Baran probably counted on both those things. But I was terrified of dying and it caused me to behave uncharitably to Lord Pal."

"Ma'am, you were under a great deal of stress," I said. "And you behaved fine."

"I did *not* behave well," the Consort said. "And I can't change the past but I can make clear my pride at being associated with your further pursuit of justice, Lord Pal. Will you wear my favor when you fight on behalf of Lady Hope?"

"If it's all right with the Leader...?" I said.

"It is," said Jon. "Lady Jolene is her own person, and I would say that even if I disagreed with her choice. Which I do not."

"I echo my friend Jon," Clain said. "I only wish I'd been back in time to fight Baran."

"In that case I'm honored to accept, your ladyship," I said to Jolene.

"Then let's return to my apartment," the Consort said. "I want to inform Lady May, and tell her I'm embarrassed not to have owned my indebtedness sooner."

Guntram and I were in the practice hall but we were using a machine which Guntram had specially modified rather than one of the fifty-odd machines ready for anybody who happened to show up. There were in fact more than a score of Aspirants working at other machines now, facing randomly generated opponents.

The one Guntram had modified for me projected simulacra of Lord Morseth. Guntram had compiled it from every time Morseth had used the machines in the hall, and had sorted the responses to pick the best counter to whatever I did. The practice machines were deceptively simple in appearance: two crystal rods slanting up from a crystal base. Ordinarily there was a plain dial control to determine the opponent's skill level.

As set, every option the device I was using offered was a simulacrum of Lord Morseth. The quick lesson I took from that is that Morseth was very bloody good. I wasn't surprised by that, but knowing that in the back of my mind was different from studying the warrior as a potential opponent whom I would have to beat.

And I was hanged as to how I was going to do that. I said to Guntram, "I'm going to go for a long session now."

He switched on the device, and I was facing my friend Morseth. He swung overhand at me; instead of guiding his blow into the ground with my weapon as I habitually would, I merely angled the shield slightly and let it take almost the full force of the stroke. I thrust for the center of his shield. The straight shot was hard enough that it must have felt warm to Morseth's left forearm behind the shield. He was uncomfortable and he'd moved away.

My equipment was as good as any in Dun Add: it was light and handy, but had the concentrated power of gear of twice the weight and bulk. The problem is that a warrior as big and strong as Morseth could handle big heavy hardware as easily as I did mine.

I thrust again for the same point. Morseth swung again as though I was a tent peg which he was driving into the ground.

My shield absorbed the blow, though I'm not sure it had ever had a workout like this before. As a matter of taste I met slashing blows with my own weapon and redirected my opponent's effort into the ground or empty air. Morseth would not expect this slogging response from me.

I prodded his shield once more in the same place. Morseth backed two steps and did something I'd never seen a warrior do before: he transferred his shield to his right hand and with the weapon in his left hand he advanced again with another overhand blow. I suppose his left arm wasn't as strong as his right, but it was sure strong enough.

I thrust again but didn't hit quite the same point because the angle had changed.

For the remainder of the round I went back to my usual technique of deflecting my opponent's blows. I switched off my gear at the end of the round and saw Lord Clain watching me from the sidelines. I called out, "Guntram, I'll wait a while before starting the next round."

Guntram obediently took the practice machine out of sequence. I turned to Clain and said, "Been watching for long, sir?"

"Most of the latest round," Clain said. "If I may ask, Lord Pal...?"

"Anything," I replied. I owed Clain deference as Chancellor

of the Commonwealth but still more as the paramount warrior of my acquaintance.

He nodded. "Were you trying to wear Morseth down initially?"

I forgot deference and barked a laugh. "No, I was not," I said. "I was attacking his shield, because unlike Morseth himself it has a failure point. He then switched hands between his weapon and shield, so not even that worked."

"You're both exceptional warriors," Clain said. "Ah, Pal. If you don't mind my asking...?"

"Anything you want to ask," I said.

"You and Lord Morseth are friends, are you not, I believe?"

"We are," I agreed.

"Is there any chance that Lord Morseth would use less than his full abilities in fighting you?" Clain asked.

"No bloody chance in the world!" I said, sounding hotter than I meant to be. Clain didn't mean to insult my friend. "To tell the truth, the problem is more the other way."

"*You* would slack off in a bout with Morseth?" Clain said, sounding incredulous.

Put that way it was nonsense. "No," I said. "But what you asked was if I'd use less than my full abilities. You saw what happened when I pecked at the same point on his shield?"

"He changed hands," Clain said, frowning.

"Yes, and while he was doing that he was open," I explained. "I'd never seen that done before and I wasn't ready for it."

"I've combined all of Morseth's combats I have access to," Guntram explained. "The only time he changed hands like that is when he was being pressed by a group of three attackers, but the device sorts among possible responses for the most suitable one."

Clain chuckled. "The device thinks you're the equivalent of three bandits, Lord Pal," he said. "And I venture that it's right."

"Three bandits, sure," I said, thinking about the guards at Allingham, "but Morseth is a friend of mine. He's open when he's changing hands but I'd have to cut his foot off to take advantage of it. That would cripple him for life if he even survived. I won't do that to a friend."

Clain considered that for a moment, then said, "You can never predict how a battle will go. But it's my opinion that if you don't defeat Morseth that way, he will kill you instead."

I grimaced. "That's pretty much what I figure too," I said. I'd been fighting his likeness all morning so I had a valid opinion.

Clain nodded instead of commenting. He knew that not all decisions were rational—or maybe my decision not to cripple Morseth *was* rational because I knew I'd have to live with the consequences.

"Who will be standing on the sidelines for you, Lord Pal?" Clain asked, as I was preparing to ask Guntram to switch on the training device again.

I laughed. "Well, at the moment I told Lady Hope I'd stand up for her, I figured to ask Morseth if he was in town."

A skilled warrior outside the actual fight could see things that the participant himself could not. I didn't need a coach in the sense of telling me how to fight, but the person in a fight wasn't in the best place to see how his opponent moved when he wasn't actually striking.

"Have you asked Reaves in Morseth's stead?" Clain asked.

"I thought about that," I said. "Reaves and I are friends, and he's not thrilled about Morseth backing Joy. Who's a nasty bitch, so far as I can see."

"There's others that feel that way about her," Clain said. "But Jon will follow the law so long as she does."

"I wouldn't have him do anything different," I said.

"Pal," Clain said. "Would you be willing to have *me* in your corner?"

"You, Lord Clain?" I repeated. "Milord, I'd be greatly honored if you were willing to do that. And if the Leader was all right with it also."

"Jon is all right," Clain said. "If the Chancellor were to appear for a party in a private matter, Jon would object, but he sees no problem with me standing on the sidelines for my friend Pal."

"Then thank you from the bottom of my heart, sir," I said.

This was the first good news I'd had since learning that Joy's Champion was Lord Morseth. It was definitely a time for good news.

CHAPTER 18

Choosing Sides

When I got back to the townhouse at noon, Fritz was still preparing lunch for three but May and her guest weren't here yet. They came in a few minutes behind me. Instead of a female friend from the palace, she was leading Lord Reaves.

"Hey, buddy," I said. "I wasn't expecting you, but I'm bloody pleased to see you."

"Yeah, May's been on me about convincing Morseth to take it easy on you," Reaves said. "You going to take up where she left off?"

"Hell, no," I said. "I'd save my breath."

Dom came down the stairs with glasses and a bottle of wine. "I'll have water with dinner, and maybe a jack of lager afterward," I said. "I've got a while to go at the hall later so I'm not drinking myself legless."

Fritz tapped the small gong at the dining room doorway, and I led the way up. "Say," I said over my shoulder to Reaves. "Say, I've been working with the machines but you wouldn't care to give me a bout for real out on the jousting ground, would you?"

"Guess I could do that," Reaves said. The practice machines were better in theory, but my experience is that a human being can respond in ways a modeled human personality will not. That level of randomness is something you've got to keep in mind in a real fight.

Add to that the fact that Reaves is very good and that he

169

partnered with Morseth in many fights made him a perfect sparring partner for somebody planning to fight Morseth in the near future.

"Pal, I want you to know," Reaves said as we all settled in the dining room upstairs. "If there was a way I could convince Morseth not to fight you I'd have done it already, but he says so long as Lady Joy wants to pursue it, he'll keep his word. There's one good thing about this—Morseth got so pissed off at the way Joy got hardass about any kind of compromise with her sister that he's not sleeping with her anymore. She's a poisonous bitch if ever there was one."

Reaves paused and put his wine cup down. "Look, Pal," he said. "You mustn't blame Morseth. He really doesn't want to fight you."

I sighed and said, "I don't blame him. I sure as hell wish that Jon had sent somebody other than a friend of mine to fetch Lady Joy back from Laferriere, though."

That was true, but I knew just why the Leader had picked Morseth and Reaves for the job. They were hard-nosed men who *would* bring Lady Joy to Dun Add regardless of her protests. Joy could not divert them from their duty regardless of what she offered. If her body could win Morseth to sympathize with her, there was nothing dishonorable about that—so far as he was concerned.

I might wish that Morseth had better taste in women, but I've thought that about plenty of other men. I was very lucky that May was as good and *nice* as she was.

CHAPTER 19

Appeal by Combat

Lord Clain was waiting for me on the jousting ground when I arrived fifteen minutes before the bout. Before we even had a moment to chat the trumpeter standing with Jon and his court at the north end of the field blew three short notes, then paused and three more: the assembly signal.

"I suppose you're being summoned to receive Lady Jolene's favor," Clain said. "Nobody discussed it with me."

"At any rate we know we're to assemble on the standard," I said. I started off for the colorful clothing on the north end.

I was honored by the Consort's notice but part of me thought of it as another bloody complication. Though—

I glanced over to Lord Morseth when I came abreast his location farther up the field. As challenger he wore black, and he looked bloody *huge.* He was a big man in all truth but I swear he'd grown since we met the night before.

"I won't wish you good luck today like I usually would," I called to him.

"The last chance of good luck was before we got into this mess," he responded.

Reaves beside him looked as miserable as if he was at his best friend's funeral. Well, that wouldn't be long coming—or near to it.

Both sisters were close by Jon now. So was Lady May in blue, what she knew was the outfit of hers I liked best. She was beautiful whatever she wore. I'd thought that the day I arrived

171

in Dun Add, and okay, you can say what kind of taste can you expect from a kid who's only seen peasant girls in a backwater like Beune?

But I'd been over a year in Dun Add, and none of the women in the court or passing through it held a candle to her.

The Consort wore red as she'd said she would.

Now she stepped close to me and took her right sleeve in her left hand and tugged sharply. The sleeve came away in her hand—it must have been just whip-stitched. She waved it in the air, facing first the east and then the west long sides of the rectangular field.

Jolene bent and brought the sleeve down to my right wrist. I opened my hand and helped her work the sleeve over my arm. It was made of flannel not muslin like the rest of her dress. I pinched a fold between my thumb and forefinger to be sure of the fabric; I met Jolene's eyes.

She said, "I was told that you'd be wetting your arm down to cool it in the course of the fight."

"Quite right," I agreed, flexing my right hand.

I was already wearing a flannel undersleeve beneath the slick bleached broadcloth of my outer garment. In a fight the warriors' equipment heated up and except for the little that dissipated in the air the warrior's hands had to absorb the heat. The fight with Lord Morseth was likely to go on for a very long time—unless I managed to lose quickly, which I hoped not to do.

I wondered if Clain had advised her on using a sleeve material that would absorb a lot of water. It might have been Jon himself. Dun Add had been a robbers' roost until Jon and Clain had cleared it to become the capital of the reborn Commonwealth. Because Jon was a lawgiver and a peacemaker, it was easy to forget that if he hadn't also been a deadly warrior, there wouldn't have been a Commonwealth to lead.

I raised my right arm high, clenched my fist, and rotated to give all the spectators a view. This sort of showmanship offended me, but it was what Jolene wanted.

Some opponents might have been impressed or even angered by the Consort's blatant support for me. I didn't expect any effect on Morseth. He would do his job in a workmanlike fashion. His job this time was to defeat Lady Hope's Champion.

Jon nodded and the trumpeter blew recall. Morseth and I

walked back to our positions on either side of midfield, Morseth a little to the north of me. I offered Sam a bucket of water, and after he drank I ducked my right arm into it, soaking both layers of flannel. I then dried my palms on my thighs and drew the shield and weapon from my tunic pockets. I didn't switch them on yet, however.

Morseth and I exchanged nods. The worst thing about this business is that we really were friends.

The trumpet blew to kick things off. I switched on the hardware and stepped forward with my weapon slightly raised because I expected Morseth to come on with an overhead cut.

That's what he did, swinging a pile-driver blow that I met with my weapon rather than taking it on my shield. I used Sam's predictive ability—dogs track motion much better than human brains can—to slant Morseth's weapon into the ground.

Even though I avoided most of the energy Morseth put into his stroke, my arm took a terrific shock. I was able to carry on as planned, however: I thrust into the center of Morseth's shield, just as I'd practiced so many times.

It didn't rock him off-balance but it wasn't what he'd expected and he didn't strike back as quickly as he might have done. When he did, it was with another overhand blow, though not quite such a powerhouse. It was still a good one to redirect rather than take on my shield. It was a very good shield, but a warrior like Morseth could batter through it if allowed to.

I pecked the center of his shield again in response. Already the focused energy of my blows must be raising the shield's temperature noticeably. Not dangerously yet, but a warrior as experienced as Morseth must have been aware of the risk.

This was a good bout for the spectators. When I met his weapon with my own, there were showers of sparks in all directions. I was very glad to have soaked my tunic sleeve before we started. I'd learned that when I fought Lord Baran. Morseth is more clever than Baran, but I swear he's even stronger as well.

My ripostes to his mighty swings were much less colorful, but I was giving blow for blow and doing damage to his equipment that he can't have expected. Morseth was wealthy and could afford the best hardware he could find. Because of his strength he could use much larger and heavier gear than I did. This may have been one of the first times his shield had been stressed to the edge of failure.

I wasn't trying to overpower Morseth or to wear him out, but I was forcing him to fight on my terms rather than his own. I'd frightened Lord Baran into thinking that because I was a Maker, I somehow had created equipment better than his. Morseth knew that his own hardware was as good as Louis himself could create, but he really respected my intelligence. When he felt his shield getting dangerously warm he feared that I'd identified a design flaw and was exploiting it.

There was no flaw. I was just hitting exactly the same point as a result of practice on Guntram's compilation. When Morseth had switched hands before his shield had been overpowered by multiple opponents.

I was alone but I was being very precise.

I suddenly realized that I could defeat Lord Morseth without any trick. He was trying to batter through my defenses. I could peck a hole in his and if I did he'd have to yield or die, and knowing Morseth I couldn't be sure of which he'd choose.

The trumpet blew the end of the round.

I took a step back and would have fallen if Lord Clain hadn't moved up to catch me.

The trumpet sounded again, a long complex call indicating the end of the match. "What's going on?" I shouted at Clain.

He'd brought the water bucket. I thrust my arm into it thankfully, then made room for Sam, who slurped water in his turn. He never overwatered himself in the middle of a battle.

"I have no bloody idea!" Clain said. "But here's the man who can tell us!"

Jon had walked over from the noble spectators. Lady Hope was with him. To my surprise, the Leader waved Lord Morseth to him also. He and Reaves stumbled over.

The ground where we'd been fighting looked like a partly plowed field from where Morseth's redirected blows had scarred the turf. *No wonder my arm feels like it went through a sausage grinder!*

"Sir," I said to Jon, speaking more politely than I had Lord Clain a moment before. "Can you tell us what's going on?"

"Right," Morseth said. "I'm not complaining, but it sure didn't seem to me that the bout was over."

"*I* ended it," said Lady Hope. "I couldn't bear to see you doing such terrible things just for money. I told Lord Jon that I resign my claim to our father's estate."

May was standing right behind Hope looking pleased. Everyone agreed that Lady Joy wasn't going to back down, so May had worked on Hope, who was just as nice as I'd thought she was.

"Lord Morseth," I said, "I declare myself beaten. I'm not capable of fighting you any longer. You win this combat."

I reached over to take his hand and found I had trouble lifting my arm and bending the fingers. Morseth reached out with difficulty. His weapon and shield were in the holsters which hung from his bandolier. I could smell leather charring.

Morseth said, "I can't let you do that, Lord Pal. My shield was on the point of failure and I couldn't go out again without committing suicide—which I didn't sign on for. I knew you were good, Pal, but I didn't know how *bloody* good you were. I cede the victory to you—and anybody who thinks I'm a wimp for saying that is welcome to challenge me and see how much of a wimp I really am! I yield."

He looked at the Leader then switched his eyes to Lady Joy, who had joined the group also—but on the other side of May, from where her sister stood.

"I don't think anyone who watched this bout," said Lord Clain, "will deny that it was the hardest fought of their experience. As it certainly was of mine."

"Wait a minute," Lady Joy said. "Hope yielded. That means I won my appeal!"

"No, milady," said Jon. "You put the matter out of your hands when you appealed to combat. At that point it became the warriors themselves who have sole jurisdiction over the matter. They have chosen to yield to one another after a duel which demonstrated their good faith. The matter is therefore in my hands to decide."

Joy appeared to be about to speak. Jon looked directly at her and spoke over the would-be interjection, "I will announce my decision at midday tomorrow in the courtroom." He turned and walked off.

Morseth moved closer with Reaves beside him and said, "Say, Pal? How about coming over to the Silver Eel with me and Reaves and get outside a couple bottles of something? Clain, I'd be glad of your company too if you'd like to come."

I looked to Lady Hope, who'd been joined by her two law clerks, Loong and Toshi, who were presumably explaining the legal situation to her. "Thanks, buddy," I said. "I'm really glad it ended this way. I think I better see my principal first, though."

"I suspect we'll be there till pretty bloody late," Morseth said, "so if you get done and want to join us, you'll still be welcome."

Waving, the two friends went off toward town.

Clain said to me, "Did you intend to force Morseth to change hands after all?"

"That's what it must have looked like," I agreed, "but no, I hadn't changed my mind. He's too good a friend to trick into letting me cripple him. But I found I could keep him back by attacking his shield, so that's what I did."

I stopped, which caused Clain to stop also. "Sir," I said. "This was a real fight, don't doubt it. I wasn't holding back and I'll tell the *world* Morseth wasn't. But I'm really glad that neither of us got killed."

Clain clasped me on the nearer shoulder. "So am I, Lord Pal."

Hope and her law clerks watched us approaching. The clerks fell silent; from what I'd seen Hope wasn't doing much talking to begin with.

I bowed and said to her, "Milady, I thank you from the bottom of my heart for halting the fight."

"Lady May told me you and Lord Morseth were good friends," Hope said. "I couldn't let you kill each other."

Your sister certainly could have, I thought. Aloud I said, "Ma'am, I think Laferriere is a wealthy node, so there was quite a bit of wealth at stake."

Hope waved her hand dismissively. "Father didn't keep us short," she said. "I have property in Dun Add, including the villa I'm living in while I visit. I'm sure Joy has just as much squirreled away as I do. I can't imagine why she's so anxious to get my share of Daddy's estate as well as her own. We've got *enough.*"

"I know what you mean," I said, "but there's plenty of folks don't see it that way. I'd guess your sister is somebody who thinks that *everything* ought to belong to her. I've met others that way."

I smiled and added, "People who think it all ought to be theirs are part of the reason I came to Dun Add to join Jon's companions."

I cleared my throat and said, "I wish I'd been able to clear things up for you."

She leaned over and kissed me lightly. "It really doesn't matter, Pal," she said. "You know, May is very lucky."

I didn't know that, but I was glad to hear it from Hope.

CHAPTER 20

Court

I entered the courtroom an hour early. There'd been a lot of spectators at the bout and I wasn't sure how full the room would be for the climax.

People drifted in slowly but in fact it never filled up. I guess there was a lot more interest in a battle between two Champions than there was in the division of an estate far from Dun Add.

I sat just behind Lady Hope and her law clerks. Toshi saw me and instantly gripped my hand. That brought Lady Hope's attention and she said, "Thank you, Lord Pal."

"I'm sorry it didn't work out better," I said.

"I'm just glad that you both survived," Hope said. "Watching the fight I didn't think that would be possible. I never would have forgiven myself if one of you had been killed."

"Ma'am," I said, "Lord Morseth and I both understood the dangers of what we were doing."

To my surprise Morseth and Reaves came down the wall-side aisle from the entrance, slid into my row, and moved all the way down until Morseth was right beside me.

I shook hands with him and said, "I just told Lady Hope that we both understood the risks of what we were doing yesterday."

"Right," said Morseth. "But we bloody well didn't understand we'd be fighting each other till we'd pledged ourselves."

"We kept our words," I agreed. "And I'll tell the world that I hope never to have this tough a fight again."

Jon entered court from the back of his box. His herald struck a triangle softly, sending a plangent note through the big room.

I noted Lady Joy sitting on the other side of the room with her clerks. I gestured to them with my thumb and tapped Morseth on the arm. He brought his lips close to my left ear and whispered, "I supported her on the field. That's all of me that she owns."

I nodded. Lord Morseth was punctilious about his duties but he cared as little as any man alive about how his actions looked. It's one of the reasons we're friends, though I'd absorbed more of my mom's attitudes toward what was *right* than he'd gotten from his upbringing.

Jon turned his head from left to right, scanning all the spectators, before he said, "In the matter of the will of Count Luther of Laferriere, I have given the affair my full attention and have consulted with clerks and trusted advisors. On this matter my Chancellor, Lord Clain, has asked to say a few words before I deliver my verdict. I therefore cede to him."

He gestured to Clain seated facing the audience a step below him to his right.

Lord Clain rose to his feet. "As the Commonwealth's Chancellor," he said, "I wouldn't normally take a position on a legal matter. I am saying that this time I will swear to defend the Commonwealth's legal system *itself* with all my strength and ability. I do not know what Jon's decision will be, but regardless I will defend it against any challenge."

He sat back down. Morseth looked at me in question. I just shrugged, because I had no more idea about what was going on than he did.

In a fight I used my dog's brain to predict the course of an opponent's blows. Clain did something else. He actually seemed to know what his opponents were thinking.

I'd fought Clain once with weapons on reduced power. He'd been incognito, checking on how good I actually was. He'd knocked me silly.

Clain turned and bowed to the Leader, then sat down.

Jon resumed, saying, "I have viewed the documents and see no option better than to reinstate the decision of the Council of Five. I therefore do so herewith. The estate of the Count of Laferriere will be divided therefore equally among his daughters as determined by commissioners appointed by the Council of Five. Are there any comments by anyone present?"

He looked straight at Lady Joy as he finished. Joy's law clerks were whispering to her. She shrugged free of them and stood up. Instead of speaking to Jon, she turned around and faced the ranks of spectators on seats above her. "Are there any men present who are willing to defend the rights of a woman alone in Dun Add?"

She was a lovely full-figured woman and probably would have gotten a taker if Lord Clain had not made it clear that going against the verdict was suicide. That was fine with me, though I'd have had no reservations about defending Lady Hope's rights against any stranger.

"So?" said Joy in a challenging voice. "If that's what passes for justice and manhood in Dun Add, I'll take myself home to Laferriere."

She started up the central aisle. The Leader called after her, "The commissioners will be along in about two weeks, Mistress Noonen tells me. I will not send a Champion to enforce their requests unless I have to."

I would have felt sorry for Joy if she hadn't been, as Reaves had said when we first discussed her, "a poisonous bitch." She'd *gotten* justice, but that isn't what she'd really wanted. She'd wanted her will to be carried out.

If Joy had been willing to compromise instead of forcing him to fight a friend, Lord Morseth would have been willing to defend her claims again. He wasn't afraid of Clain—though I thought and he probably did too—that Clain would beat him.

I thought again about how fortunate I was to have May. Her existence protected me from the likes of Lady Joy.

When she passed out of the courtroom it began to buzz. Morseth said, "I guess that's all we'll hear of her."

"Unless you're tapped to back up the commissioners again," I said. I clasped hands with Lady Hope. "Guess it worked out all right after all, ma'am," I said. "I'm going over to chat with May, who came in a minute ago with all her court ladies."

CHAPTER 21

Later

The Consort had a small garden outside her suite. Plants and even some small trees grew there in pots. I took May out there when the Consort's entourage and I left the courtroom together. May hugged me and said, "Good result."

"Yes," I said. "I became a Champion to bring justice. I didn't realize that might mean fighting as good a friend as Lord Morseth."

May felt me stiffen and stepped back. "You beat him," she said.

"Not really," I said. "We yielded to each other. That might not have happened."

"Dear," May said firmly, "you achieved justice. It was dangerous and could have ended badly, but without you, there would have been injustice."

"Love, you don't like the things I do as a Champion," I said. "You've said that!"

"I like the result," she said. "I was biting my knuckles the whole time, but it was the right thing to do even against Morseth."

She put her hands on my shoulders. "Look, I'd like you to spend more time in Dun Add and I'd like us to give more parties. But I want to live in civilization, and because of men like you, I do. Quit and stay home if you like—but never think that what you do isn't as important as you thought when you were a kid!"

I kissed her. "Thank you, love," I said. "But sometimes it's very hard."

"I didn't fall in love with a soft man," she said, and kissed me back.